SURRENDER

Prey

Kendra Mei Chailyn

DEDICATION

For Adnan and Payal – May life be the ship of your dreams and love be the star you sail her by.

Dearest Lacey

Thank you so much for being you and for your support

♡ always,

Kendra Mei Chaitya

ACKNOWLEDGMENTS

Cover design by:
Kate Reedwood

Front Cover Model: A.D

Editing: Kadian Tracey

Chapter One

Owning her own business meant Shane Teller should have been able to leave whenever she wished. There were plenty she could be doing, rather than sitting in the store trying to get things figured out. It wasn't until after her wedding dress boutique became the talk of the town, that she realized running a business was a lot like having super powers—it came with responsibilities.

Leaving early, as the boss, was a myth and she'd like to meet the jerk who started it. It made absolutely no sense, especially if there was only one employee. Her only worker was a university student and couldn't be there until well after lunch. She'd work from around lunchtime until closing. Shane had toyed with the idea of hiring someone else to help out, but she wanted to keep the shop quaint.

Shane glanced at the time once more and frowned. Two minutes had passed since the last time she checked. Instead of sitting around, she busied herself with logging the new designs. There was so much to do with a new shipment, from checking to make sure nothing was damaged, to taking pictures and sending them off to the webmaster so they could be added to the website. Every little thing had to be considered. No details were too small and nothing left to chance. The last order was a big one—Vera Wang had a new line and Shane had fallen for each and every one of the dresses. Those she hadn't ordered to sell from her store were still being shown just in case a bride wanted something not on the rack.

Adding to that excitement, was a batch of amazing Rivini that were spoken for the moment people found out the designer had a new line. Those she handled with kid gloves since they were special orders. They cost a fortune and a half and damaging even the showroom pieces would make her cry. Those she sold at discounted prices at a major trunk sale at the convention center at the end of the year.

See? No stones left unturned. No dress left without a home.

Buried in tulle, chiffon and lace, Shane passed the day from sunrise to just after lunch stocking the store room, fixing the displays and catering to appointments for soon to be brides. When the bell jangled a little after one, Shane had one hand holding a ham on rye sandwich, the other tapping away at numbers on a calculator. She looked up with a smile though she wasn't expecting another client for three hours. Her only employee, Anisa walked in with a bounce to her step.

"Hi boss lady!" Anisa Ahmedagine called cheerfully. "It's a beautiful day!"

Shane laughed. "I wouldn't know. I've been in here all day trying to get the new designs up and ready to be seen."

"You know you didn't have to do all that. I'll only have three appointments in the evening I could've done it."

"Yes, but I figured since you have to deal with the Brightman party, I'd help you."

Anisa sighed. "I guess."

"And I know you have reading so on your down time, maybe catch up?"

Anisa sighed again, this time a lot more dramatically than before. "Reading—blech."

Shane laughed.

"Even with all that, nothing will ruin this day for me."

"Oh? Should I ask why?"

"Yes." She giggled. "Go ahead. Ask me why this day is so *epically* awesome!"

"Epically? I'm pretty sure that word doesn't mean what you think it means."

Anisa groaned. "Work with me here!"

"Okay." Shane gave in. "Why is this day so *epically* awesome?"

"I have a date tomorrow night!" She flailed

and did a ballerina twirl. "Can you believe it?"

"Congratulations!"

"Thank you! Guess who with."

"Michelle Porter?"

"Yes!" Anisa stopped to have a happy, almost dazed look in her eyes before she walked behind the counter to stash her bag and to adjust her hijab by looking at her reflection in a metal surface. "She said she heard from a friend that I was into girls and she had to be sure before she asked."

"Well this *is* good news! I'm very happy for you."

"Thanks—I'm nervous though."

"Nervous? You've wanted this girl to ask you out for a year now," Shane said.

"You know that saying *be careful what you wish for*? I've waited all this time and now I feel like my heart wants to jump out of my chest. What do I do?"

Shane stopped the calculations she'd been working on and faced her young employee.

Anisa had no one. After she came out as lesbian her parents disowned her and took everything. She went from having all the luxuries in the world, to living on the street. Shane couldn't have that. She framed Anisa's beautiful face with her palms and smiled into the worried eyes of her young friend. "Listen, one day at a time," Shane told her. "This is new skin you're in and though I'm proud of you, you must know relationships take time and patience. The best advice I can give you is, be you. You're adorable and caring and funny—be that. Every woman wants those things, gay or straight."

Anisa bowed her head as her cheeks pinkened. "I don't know about all that."

"Trust me." Shane grinned, releasing her face. "Want us to order a pizza to celebrate?"

"A celebratory pizza?"

"Hey, don't knock it till you've tried it."

Anisa giggled but nodded.

"Good. You order it and I'll finish this math." Shane went back to her work.

Anisa was a vegetarian even though she didn't really follow the religious thing too hard, she stayed away from meats, wore her hijab and prayed.

"Okay," Anisa said.

Shane wanted to leave Anisa with as little to do as possible. The Brightman party was a nightmare to deal with since the two mothers were always battling to see who would outdo the other. If one liked a dress, the other, even though sometimes Shane could see they both adored it, would reject it. Shane knew they were getting on the bride's nerves but she stayed out of it. If Anisa started complaining then Shane would put her foot down and tell both the old biddies to either shut up or get out. Of course, she'd say it in a polite *I'm sorry we don't seem to have the dress to satisfy your needs* way.

When she finally pushed on her sunglasses, gave Anisa a hug and darted out the door, Shane figured she was free and clear. Then her cell rang and after checking the screen she knew that wasn't true.

"Shane Teller?" she said.

"You know it's me," her sister Francine said. "Don't you *professional* me."

"Um, sorry. I didn't check the screen before I picked up. What's up, hon?"

"You've been acting weird lately. I want to know why."

"I am?" Shane asked, shoving her designer purse and catalogues from new designer houses into the back seat. She then dragged a palm over her forehead. "I'm sorry. I've just had a lot going on. We got some new deliveries plus I'm freaking out over the partnership we're running with the local fashion design school—it's been strenuous to say the least."

"Do you have a new man?"

Shane frowned as she tossed her body behind the wheel. "Sis, seriously? You know there aren't any men knocking down my door. Really, it's just work stuff. Listen, I do want to talk to you about something though but I want to have some stuff done first before I say anything."

"What about?"

"Franny, gimme until tomorrow evening at about, this time. I will call you and we'll have a chat. I don't want to say anything until I'm sure."

Francine sighed. "Okay fine. But if you don't call I'll put out an APB on your car."

"Oh lawd, really?"

Shane knew her cop sister wouldn't hesitate to do that too.

"I mean it."

"I know. I love you."

"Uh-huh," Francine said. "Love you too. But only cause I have to."

Shane giggled. They'd been saying that to each other for years. It was a running joke in the house as children and as adults it merely stuck. With the conversation over, she dropped the phone on the passenger seat, started the ignition and peeled from the parking lot.

It was just before rush hour so the only snags were red lights from Koler County to the center of Hillenue. The closer she got to her destination the more her heart raced. It was so bad at times, she had to pull over to take deep breaths. Finally, she eased her Rolls-Royce Wraith up beside her friend's Bentley, grabbed her purse and hurried into the building.

"Shane!" Jana cheered. The petite woman hurried over to kiss both her cheeks. "I've finally gotten you to come on in!"

Shane laughed. "Yeah. I figure it's time."

"Don't worry. You will look *stunning*! You will not believe how gorgeous the whole thing will be!"

Shane still wasn't convinced but she smiled and allowed Jana to walk her into the luxurious, private back space. After setting her purse down in Jana's office, Shane followed her friend's instructions on getting prepared. She stripped down and checked her body in the mirror. Noticing a few dry spots on her skin, she rushed for her purse, grabbed her lotion and hurried back into the change room. It took a couple of minutes but she managed to get her skin moisturized.

Jana entered later with a whole host of things from hair products to makeup. It took a little over forty five minutes but when Shane looked in the mirror again she couldn't believe how good she looked.

"Wow," Shane said. "I look so good…"

"See?" Jana grinned from behind her. "What'd I tell you? Wait until you see the pictures."

What followed was a photoshoot session Shane enjoyed immensely. After two years of Jana asking to shoot her, Shane finally gave in. Honestly, she didn't think she was sexy. Her body had curves in places supermodels didn't. She had flab in other places, her thighs touched, her arms had a little bit of a jiggle—Shane didn't see herself as particularly pretty.

"You want to see them now or wait until I go through?" Jana asked as Shane slipped back into her clothes.

"I'll wait. I'm in no rush. Do you know when you can send them?"

"Tonight. I left this whole evening open for you, my friend. I've been waiting for this for what feels like forever!"

Shane giggled. "Thanks, Jana. You make a girl feel wanted."

"Well, I keep telling you the men you see are idiots but you never listen to me."

"What men?" Shane sat to slip her feet back into her shoes. "They hear the name and run screaming and even if they don't run then, they take off when they hear I sell wedding dresses. And that's if they come in the first damn place." Shane stood and smoothed her hands over her hips. "Besides, I find I'm happier this way."

Jana sighed. "I have a friend…"

"No. No way. No set ups." Shane hugged her. "Shoot me an email later with the pictures. I have to head home. I promised Falcon and Danielle I would make some steamed snappers for them tomorrow. I still have to buy the fish."

"What about Falcon?"

"What *about* him?"

"Shane, the man is sexy as hell. He obviously adores you—have you ever stopped to think maybe the two of you could be something more than friends?"

Shane blinked at Jana for a few silent moments before doubling over in laughter. She laughed until her lungs burned and her sides hurt. She eve snorted. She tumbled back into the chair trying to catch her breath and shook her head.

"What? It's not funny." Jana sounded incredulous.

"Yes it is." Shane inhaled. "Do you see the women Falcon dates? Legs for days, blond hair, blue eyes, size zeros. Banners under which I'm not even in the same zip code." Shane hugged Jana. "I'll talk to you later."

"Fine. I was only suggesting."

"I know hon. See you soon."

Jana kissed her cheek and Shane left the

building still chuckling to herself about her and Falcon being anything more than friends.

Darkness had fallen over Hillenue by that time. The sun was long gone and the temperature dipped slightly. Shane loved it when it wasn't overly hot, in fact, she had to be one of the only people who left her bedroom windows open during the winter time. Artificial heat made her throat and eyes scratchy.

The moon sat in the sky like a giant piece of cheese, round and yellow, glowing over everything it reached. Traffic had thinned out since rush hour but still a bit slow on the highway.

Shane turned on the radio to jam to SonReal followed by Sebell until she could exit and went south. Her first stop was at the local West Indian market to gather the ingredients she required for the steamed Snappers. She had the gentleman at the counter clean the fish for her because she had no intentions of going home to do that.

Her next detour was to pick up an ice-cream cake to celebrate Danielle's foray back into Rugby at school and after a brief stop to grab some sparkling wine for Danielle and actual wine for the adults, she headed home.

Falcon hadn't called her all day. That worried her. He worked as the captain of the local Elite Tactical Force, a group of highly trained, mostly ex military, cops who got called in during hostage situations or other kind of jobs SWAT couldn't pull off. The team was leant out to other cities around the area and sometimes other states. During those times when Falcon was away, his daughter, Shane's God-daughter, spent the time with Shane. Shane didn't mind having her, for the seventeen year old was the closest she'd ever get to having a child of her own.

Sadness swam in on her then and threatened to overwhelmed her. Instead of allowing that to happen, she dumped her purchases, dropped the fish into water mixed with lemon juice then got her phone. Scrolling through the contacts, she stopped on Falcon and hit send.

"Hey you!" Falcon James answered after the first ring. "How are you?"

"Don't hey me." Shane pouted even though she knew he couldn't see her. "All day, Birdman? Really?"

"Sorry. I had a hell of a day and afterward I just spent it with Danielle."

"Everything okay?"

"Yeah. Nothing a beer and a hug can't cure."

"Birdman?"

"Hmmm?"

"What happened?"

Falcon cleared his throat. "Walked into a trap today."

"Shit! Are you okay?" Shane exclaimed.

"I'm fine!" Falcon assured her. "This is why I didn't want to make a big deal out of it. I just managed to extricate myself from Danielle's arms I don't need you freaking out too."

Shane smiled. "I'm sorry. How did that

happen?"

"I have no idea." Falcon sounded disheartened.

"You *are* going to find out."

"Hell yes. Someone put a target on my people's backs. I won't take that lying down. I didn't want to tell her but I have a bruise the size of an island on my chest where the vest stopped a bullet. So every time I move it hurt."

"Stay home tomorrow—lay down and rest. We can do the dinner some other time."

"No." Falcon sounded defiant. "Elle has been looking forward to this. Besides, you have a comfy sofa. I can chill there."

Shane knew arguing with Falcon never ended with her winning, especially when it came to following through on a promise. Giving up, since he was okay, she took a breath and wandered into her bedroom to change. They talked for a little while longer and after telling him what she'd bought and had planned, he went back to Danielle and she made her way back downstairs to season the fish.

It took some time to finish all the preparations for their dinner the next day. Since the plan was to have Danielle come over first thing in the morning and spend the day with her. They wouldn't be home—a girls' day of getting their nails done, hair done and a little shopping was in order to Falcon's horror. She finally entered her office and turned on the computer. The first thing she saw after opening her email, was one from Jana. Shane swallowed a lump in her throat.

"Wow…okay." She whispered, clicking on it.

One by one she opened the pictures and stared at them at length. There were seventeen of them and when she was finished, Shane had to admit they were tactfully done. None of her undesirable attributes were hanging out. "I actually look like a woman. So what the hell is the issue?"

With a sigh, she decided not to wait for the next day and put her sister out of her misery. She quickly forwarded the email to Francine after saving the images for herself. After all that, Shane sent an email to Jana asking if she could get enlarged copies of a selected few, framed for the house—the bedroom to be exact.

She took a shower then, wrapped in a towel, hair wet on her shoulders, she sat on the bed, grabbed the phone and called Francine.

"Hello?"

"Franny. Hey."

"How are you?" Francine asked.

"I'm okay. Did you get the email I sent you?"

"Um..." There was silence followed by the sound of Francine tapping away at her keyboard. "Nope. No email yet."

"That's not right—I sent it like an hour ago. Lemme check."

"Maybe the gremlins got it," Francine offered. "Send it again."

"Okay. Gimme a sec." Shane climbed from her bed to grab the laptop rather than going all the way downstairs for the computer. She opened up the email and though Francine told her to just send it again, she had to check to see if she could figure out what happened to the last one she sent. Sometimes when she forward stuff, she accidentally hit reply rather than forward and she'd send the email back to the person who sent it to her.

"Oh shit." Shane suddenly couldn't breathe. "Shit! Shit! Shit!"

"Shane?"

"No!" She continued. It was as if in that moment all she could get out was *shit* and *no.* Every other word became lodged in her throat cutting off her breathing. "Oh no!"

"Shane Colleen Teller!"

"I sent them to the wrong person!"

"Okay. Then send them an email saying it was a mistake, please ignore and move on."

"It's not that simple!"

"Sweetie, it's just an email."

Shane sent them once more, this time she ensured it went to Francine.

"Hold on, I just got an email from you…."

Shane waited, but it was as if she was stuck in molasses. Her head ached fiercely from all the adrenaline being pumped through her and her fingers had become numb from how tightly she held the phone.

"Oh girl you look scrumptious!" Francine cheered. "Who'd you send these to?"

"Falcon."

"Oh!"

"Yes! What am I going to do?"

"Just tell him you're sorry. Explain that alcohol was involved."

Shane frowned. "That's not true. I can never look at him again."

"Now you're just being dramatic."

"Am I?" Shane asked. "Your best friend hasn't seen your naughty bits."

"Shane, you don't have anything hanging out. There's no naughty bits to see."

"Oh my God."

"What're you going to do?" Francine asked.

"Throw away a twenty year friendship over a few photos? It's not like you're naked in any of them."

But her sister's words didn't help. Falcon and Danielle were coming over first thing in the morning and she wasn't sure what to do. How could she send the email to Falcon and not Francine? There were only two people with F names in her address book and she hadn't been paying attention—that was how.

"I never wanted Falcon to see me like that."

"Like what?"

"You know—exposed."

"Girl, please. I'm sure he's seen women in less," Francine said. "You're putting way too much thought into this. Tell him you didn't mean to and let's move on already. He's your friend and he loves you. I'm pretty sure he won't go apeshit. And—and, he hasn't been into women since he's been the sole parent for Danielle."

"You're right. I'll him I meant to send it to

you. I wasn't paying close enough attention and it was an accident."

"Right. Now, get some sleep. But damn girl, you are sexy!"

Shane pressed her head forward to the laptop and groaned. "Stop saying that? Especially after who else is seeing these pictures right now and I'm seeing him tomorrow."

Francine giggled.

"Oi. Love you."

"Love you too."

CHAPTER TWO

Shane barely got any sleep the night. The whole night was spent having nightmares about Falcon's reaction to the images from her boudoir photoshoot. None of the possible ways he could respond was any good. All of them ended with her in a corner sobbing.

Each nightmare caused her to jerk upright in bed covered in cold sweat. Though the window was open and the night was cool, she climbed out and turned on the air conditioner. Afterward there was no sleeping.

Bright and early, she was up, showered and dressed in a blue MXM dress that hugged her curves and went down just below her knees. She would pair that with a lacey sandals once it was time to head out. She made some breakfast, packed some in a carry away container for

Falcon and set out a couple of plates so her and Danielle could eat. Even through all of that, Shane kept reliving the horrible dreams from the night before.

A quote from the book *Shantaram* filled her head the entire night and through making food that morning—*a dream is a place where a wish and a fear meet. When the wish and fear are exactly the same, we call the dream a nightmare.* As her night phased into her morning, Shane couldn't help thinking that the character Didier in this book was full of crap. She feared what would happen between her and Falcon when they meet after he'd seen the photos. But she didn't wish she could be more than friends with him.

Then again she could fear his reaction and wish he hadn't seen those pictures—that was the only way Didier's words could ring true.

"Nope, full of crap." She muttered, closing a tin of Spicy Cinnamon Chai tea Danielle was addicted to.

Around nine, she heard the engine to

Falcon's truck pull into her driveway. Her heart instantly started racing and she couldn't dry her palms against her thighs fast enough.

When someone knocked, Shane must have jumped a foot in the air before smoothing her palms over her curves again. It took her two steps toward the entrance to remember she had packed some food for Falcon. Quickly, she hurried back to the kitchen, grabbed it and wandered to the door and pulled it open.

"Good morning Godie," Danielle said, reaching in for a hug.

"Hey hon." Shane managed. "You guys are early." She glanced by Danielle's head to see Falcon had his arms folded over his chest, his ankles crossed and was leaning into the side of his vehicle. He stared back at Shane with something unreadable in his eyes and that was new to Shane. "Hey you." She waved at Falcon. "What's up?"

"Hi. I can't stay," Falcon said.

"I know." Shane shrugged. "You had an

appointment."

"He has a mission," Danielle explained. "We're on our own until he gets back."

"I said I was sorry," Falcon said. "You know these bad-guys have no respect for my personal time."

Danielle dropped her bags inside and ran back to hug her father. He dropped a small kiss to her lips and smoothed her hair from her face before allowing her to return to the house.

"Do you know what time you'll be back?" Shane asked.

Falcon shook his head. Shane, though terrified of what he'd say, descended the front stairs to stand beside him. "You saw them, right?"

"Yeah."

"And we're going to have to talk about them." Shane didn't know how she managed to remain standing.

"At some point," Falcon replied. "But not now."

"I figured. I'm sorry. I meant to send them to…"

"Francine. I know."

"I'm really sorry." She offered him the warm container.

Falcon kissed her head and stepped away to open the door to climb in. "Don't worry about it. I'll be back as soon as I can."

"Okay."

"Thanks for this." Falcon lifted the sealed bowl toward her.

Shane managed to give him a small smile before joining Danielle on the top step and waved to Falcon until the truck was long gone. It took a second to get herself unglued from the spot she'd been standing in, but when Danielle wrapped an arm around her hips, she returned the gesture and walked with her God-daughter into the house and closed the door. Though they had to reheat breakfast, they finally sat down to eat.

"So, how's school?" Shane asked.

"Okay, I guess. It's getting harder and harder because they're pushing us toward university and college."

"Do you have any idea where you'd like to go?"

Danielle bit into a piece of dumpling and took a breath. "I wanted to go to Hillenue University for Fashion Design but I don't know. Dad said he'd be happy if I followed my heart but Fashion Design may be a little, you know, embarrassing for him."

"Why'd you say that?"

"Well, look at his life. He has a bachelor in Police Foundations with a minor in psychology." Danielle stopped speaking to take a healthy swallow from her orange juice. "He has an Associates that he got while fighting mom in court and he's the head of an elite strike force unit. Your sister is a detective! How cool is that? You own your own business with an education to match—and I'd just be a fashion designer."

"Don't think that way." Shane leaned over to

smooth a hand over her dark, brown hair. "Your father loves you and if you want to design clothes for a living or sell hot dogs on the street, he'd be happy."

"Are you sure?"

"I'm sure. Besides, I own my own wedding dress business. Sure, I won't be doing it forever but I have connections that when it comes time for your internship, I can pull a few strings. Whatever you chose to do, make sure it's something that makes you happy and you work hard to be the best at it."

Danielle's face lit up. Her hazel eyes shimmered excitedly before she darted around the table to hug Shane tightly. "Thanks Godie."

"Oh you're welcome darling." She hung onto Danielle a little longer than she probably should, but her eyes were burning with unshed tears and she didn't want Danielle to see that. Once she was under control again, Shane released Danielle and they finished breakfast.

All through the day, even with the fun she

was having, even with the love she felt for Danielle, Shane couldn't help thinking back to the way Falcon had stared at her from the truck. She even found herself admiring the easy way he relaxed into the hard metal of the vehicle. At one point while Danielle went into the change room to try on a gothic looking jacket, Shane allowed herself the fantasy of watching Falcon strip. Immediately, she caught herself and felt horrible for even letting her thoughts go there.

With numerous bags, Shane resigned herself to being God-mother mama, as Danielle often called her, for the day and enjoy Danielle's company. They talked and laughed and people watched. And just before heading back home with their nails and hair done, the two stopped for Beavertails at a food truck in the city. They then hurried back to Shane's place and while Danielle called her best friend to regale him with tales of the day, Shane hurried into the kitchen to begin cooking. They'd spent an extra hour on the street and were behind.

Once their suspect was in custody and the paperwork filed, Falcon James debriefed his team and hurried down to the change room with his other best friend, Topaz Chen, on his heels. The two met in the SEALS Falcon's second year in. For a while neither man spoke. That was the way things were after the adrenaline wore off. In those moments as they changed back into their civilian clothes, it seemed they used that time to contemplate their humanity.

"I saw some pictures of Shane last night," Falcon finally spoke.

"You have tons of pictures of her, man," Topaz said then pointed. "There are three in your locker right now. Hell, you have at least two in your wallet. What's the big deal?"

"You know this trend going around where women go out and have steamy photos of themselves taken? Not naked but hot enough to singe your eyebrows off?"

Topaz laughed then arched a brow.

"Wait…no!"

"Yes." Falcon finished with his belt then sat down to haul on his boots. "And I have to tell you, they were so hot I got hard."

"Let me guess, you feel bad."

"Of course! Wouldn't you?" Falcon tugged the laces in place and drew them tightly into a bow. "There was especially this one with her in nothing but a pair of silver stilettos and an oversized Hillenue Bravos jersey top. I'm telling you, Paz."

"Okay. Let's talk this out."

"I'm not one of our suspects."

"That's not the point. You obviously are worked up about this so let's talk. How'd you get the pictures?"

"She meant to send them to her sister…"

"Francine?"

"Yeah. I guess she wasn't paying attention and sent them to me." Falcon stood and took a breath before reaching in to grab his badge. "I was curious as to what she meant when she said *let me know what you think of these pictures* so I opened them. I know nothing could ever happen between us because she's my best friend. I've known her since she was a little girl and Shane would never look at me as anything more than good old Birdman."

"You sound bitter."

"I'm not bitter." Falcon inhaled deeply, held it before releasing the breath out his mouth. "Frustrated—and horny. There's a difference."

Topaz closed his locker and sighed. "Didn't they say before you marry someone you should be friends first? Let's deal in what we know, right? Danielle *adores* Shane. We know that she's been more of a mother to your baby than her own mother. We know Shane cares about you. She worries about you. She brings us the *best* cheesecakes for our raffles. And now we know she turns you on."

"Don't say it like that."

"Falco, listen," Topaz said. "Do you know how long I've been looking for a good woman?

So she doesn't look at you like a lover now, but you can seduce her, show her that if she only opens her eyes and give you a chance you could not only rock her world but you'd keep doing it for the rest of your lives."

"I don't believe in that. Look how well the first marriage ended."

"Remember on your wedding day what I asked you?"

Falcon remembered it perfectly. Topaz had walked into the groom suite with a grim look on his face, sat Falcon down and asked him, "are you sure?"

"Of course I'm sure." Falcon had been incredulous.

"Don't get pissy at me. I'm your best man, I'm supposed to ask you this."

Falcon nodded to bring himself back to the present.

"I didn't ask you that because I was trying to be an asshole." Topaz continued. "I asked because I didn't particularly like Shannon, you know this. But I tolerated her because she was the love of your life. Shane, I like."

"Because of the cheesecakes?"

Topaz laughed. "Yes and because she doesn't let you get away with anything and she takes care of you and my God baby."

Falcon pushed a loud breath out his mouth and finished getting dressed. He shoved his gun into his holster then drew on his coat around it. "I have to get going," he said. "Shane is making dinner tonight for me and the kidlet. We're celebrating her making it onto the rugby team."

"Oh yeah? What position?"

"Back."

"Yes! I've seen that child run."

Falcon chuckled and extended a closed fist to Topaz. "See you later. If there's any cheesecake, I'll save you a piece."

"Don't tease me." Topaz touched his fist to Falcon's.

Finally alone with his thoughts, Falcon climbed back into his truck and made his way toward Shane's place. He had a change of clothes with him so he figured he could take a shower there. He kept reliving the moment he first saw the picture of Shane in his favorite team's jersey. For years, he'd slept in the same bed as Shane, gone skinny dipping with Shane, walked into the bathroom while she showered and never once did he think anything sexual. Sure, after she began spending more time with Danielle he found himself wondering if she could love him like a lover but never anything pornographic.

At her place, Danielle let him in the house as Shane was on the phone with her employee about a client. He stopped at the door to blow her a kiss then headed upstairs to shower. He used the one in her bedroom because the other shower was too small for his six foot frame. Once he was clean, he got dressed in a graphic t-shirt, a pair of jeans and walked barefoot down the steps to find his daughter setting the table. He kissed her nose.

"How was today?"

"Good," he replied, helping her with wine glasses.

"Godie got me sparkling wine so I get to use one of those glasses," Danielle told him when he skipped her spot with the wine tumblers.

"She did?" Falcon asked, his heart rising. Who else would have done that? "I like it."

Danielle laughed. "How is your chest?"

"Still a little sore but I'm still standing."

"I worry about you, dad," Danielle admitted.

Falcon stared at her for a moment before hugging her tightly. "Would you like me not to do this anymore?"

"Don't be silly, dad." Danielle walked out of his arms to set a large jug full of lemonade in the center of the table. "This is what you love. All I need you to do is promise me you'll be careful."

"I promise."

"I mean it."

Falcon smiled and pushed a wayward strand of hair behind her ear. "Me too."

"Okay you two," Shane said, entering the

space. "Sorry about that. We have a client from hell and I just gave Anisa permission to tell her to find another store. Her mother and mother in law are Satan and his concubine."

Danielle giggled.

Falcon covered his daughter's ears.

"I heard that," Danielle said, looking up into Falcon's eyes. "And I know what concubine means. I read books."

Falcon groaned but released her ears. She walked into the kitchen and Shane followed her. Shane still had fear in her eyes and that broke Falcon's heart. All their lives he never wanted to have her look at him as if he'd hurt her. He wanted to grab her arm, to stop her, to explain that he didn't mind getting the pictures. Then again that could freak her out even more—especially since she only saw him as a friend. But he shoved his fingers deeply into his pockets to stop himself. What Falcon needed was a chance to get over what he'd seen. He frowned while accepting a salad bowl from Shane. He had as much chance of unseeing her curves decked out in six inch heels, high-waist panties, a string of pink pearls and an arm covering her voluptuous breasts as getting hit by lightning.

Shit. First step, stop thinking of her boobs – voluptuous or otherwise.

He made a couple more trips, dancing around his daughter who hummed while she helped to set the table and once everything was ready, they sat together to eat. Shane sat across from him while Danielle took her usual spot at the head of the table. Danielle went on and on about her team and how happy she was to be a part of it. Falcon watched the interaction between his daughter and her God mother and rarely put in a word or two here and there. For the most part he was just content to see his daughter so lit up and Shane so interested.

With dinner over, Falcon was surprised when Shane brought out the chocolate cake while singing *For She's a Jolly Good Lady* instead of fellow. He laughed and joined in singing with her. Danielle applauded before flailing and snagging a desert plate and a knife.

"Okay, since it's your cake, you cut and serve," Falcon said.

Danielle readily did as he suggested and when she finally sat down to her slice, he watched the way she cut off a piece and slowly stuck it into her mouth. She groaned. "Okay, this is good," she approved.

Soon, the festivities were over and while Danielle took some time to call her best friend and gush to him about her evening, Falcon worked silently beside Shane to stock the dishwasher.

"This is stupid," Shane said. "We were never the friends to not have anything to say to each other."

"I agree."

"Okay, let's talk about these dumb pictures and get it out of the way, okay?"

Falcon dried his hands on a dishtowel and nodded. "Okay."

"I just wanted something to make me feel like a woman." Shane started but she didn't look at him. In fact, she seemed to go out of her way not to let their gazes meet. "I'm not exactly the sexiest woman alive so men haven't exactly flocked to my feet if you know what I mean. Jana finally talked me into letting her shoot me and for an hour I felt desirable."

"Shane…"

"I know you didn't want to see all of that." Shane continued like he hadn't even spoken. "And I don't blame you for being upset. The only people that I intended to see those photos were me, Jana and Franny."

"Shane…"

"It's just, I wasn't paying attention and I was nervous about what Franny would say and…"

Falcon grabbed her shoulders and spun her to face him. "Shane!"

"What?"

"Stop talking."

"Wha…" She blinked up at him, her brown

eyes filled with unshed tears. Falcon shook his head and released her shoulders, eve managing to take a step away from her without toppling over. "I told you, it's fine. Besides, you look good in them."

Shane tilted her head.

"I don't know why you're so down on yourself," Falcon said. "So a few guys are idiots? There is a man out there for you."

But even as he said those words he could imagine running said man over with his car. The rage about that one sentence filled him so quickly and completely, he shook his head and arched a brow. "The pictures didn't offend me," Falcon said, then paused to measure his words. How much should he really admit to her? "And it's not like you were naked in any of them."

"Naked? Oh lawd never! Jana's camera would explode."

Falcon chuckled and opened the dishwasher to drop a wayward fork in. "Maybe."

"Maybe?" Shane laughed and bounced him

with her hip. "You're supposed to say *no my beauty. Never!*"

"No, my beauty. Never!"

"Now you're just being an ass." She chided with a pout.

Falcon tapped her protruding lips with an index finger and grinned. "I thought that was what you wanted to hear. Women are complicated."

Shane wiggled her brows at him and started the dishwasher. When they exited the kitchen, they found Danielle fast asleep, still on the phone with Charlie. Falcon picked up the phone.

"Hello?" he said.

"Hey Mr. James. She fell asleep again?"

"Yeah."

Charlie laughed. "I told her to hold on because I had to use the bathroom. Oh well, I'll talk to her tomorrow."

"All right. Goodnight, Charlie."

"Night."

Falcon hung up the phone and dropped it in

her purse that was sitting on the floor.

"She's asleep?" Shane asked.

Falcon looked up toward the door. "Yup. Out like a light." He hunched down beside her to watch her face. It was scary how much she looked like her mother. He wondered how many other traits she inherited from Shannon. Though he disliked his ex-wife, his heart overflowed at the mere thought of Danielle. He didn't understand it nor did he spend time questioning it.

"You guys should spend the night," Shane said.

Falcon glanced at her over his shoulder. She had a blue shawl wrapped around her shoulders and was leaning into the doorframe. Falcon wanted to tell her it wasn't a good idea, that all he wanted to do was kiss the lines the light behind her was making against her cheeks and neck. But to cover him staring, Falcon smiled and scooped Danielle into his arms. "I'll take her up to the room. I'll crash on the couch."

"There's no need for that." Shane frowned. "We've always shared my bed when Danielle sleeps over. It's still the same bed."

Falcon's heart raced terribly at that thought. Again, if he declined the idea she'd know something was wrong. With a curt nod, he carried his daughter by her and up the stairs. With the moonlight as his guide, he set Danielle on the bed, removed her slippers and pulled the sheets up to her neck. He kissed her head, smoothed her hair back then left the room and closed the door behind him.

Back downstairs, he watched Shane type away for a second before clearing his throat. She looked up and smiled at him.

"I have a few emails to send before I go to bed," Shane said. "You turning in?"

"I'm not tired." It was a lie. Falcon was exhausted. Even so, he knew with her lying beside him he wouldn't get a wink of sleep.

"Wanna watch a movie?"

"No romantic crap."

Shane laughed. "When have I ever done that to you?"

"Sex and the City one. Sex and the City two…"

"My bad." Shane giggled, closing her laptop. "Okay, fine. We'll watch something funny—what'd you say?"

Falcon agreed and followed her up the stairs to her bedroom. While she brushed her teeth, he stood by the window wondering why he couldn't just put himself out of his misery and sleep the sofa. Then again, it wasn't long enough for his frame and it would be hell on his back in the morning.

"Birdman, can you pick a movie?" Shane called from the bathroom. "It has to be something funny. I got that new on demand channel."

"Okay," Falcon replied. He grabbed the remove and sat on the side of the bed. Once he was on the on demand channel, he scrolled through the movie listing and settled on Monty

Python and the Holy Grail. He'd heard it was funny but hadn't had a chance to see it yet. "How about Monty Python?"

"Yes."

"Um…" Falcon tilted his head. "But you don't know which one."

"Don't care. As long as it's Monty Python the answer is yes."

Falcon shook his head. "What's your passcode?"

"14236."

He typed it in and paused the movie for her to come back. By the time she did, he was shirtless and lying with his back propped up against a pillow on the headboard. He'd found a book on her bedside table and was browsing it. It was erotica. She stepped from the bathroom wearing pajamas with unicorn on them. He smiled and shook his head.

"What?"

"Nothing. Come on."

"You don't like my PJs?"

Falcon grinned. "I like. I like. Can we watch the movie now?"

Shane climbed into bed, under the blankets and he remained on top. They both turned off their respective lamps and he fumbled around in the dark to find the remote. Soon the movie was playing and though he found it funny, he wasn't really paying attention. He was a little busy desperately trying to keep his body from overheating.

Luckily, Shane fell asleep before the movie ended. He climbed out of the bed and made his way to the couch. He was aroused by her and if he wanted to get any sleep that night, bad back the next morning or not, he couldn't stay with her in that giant king bed.

CHAPTER THREE

Being late is something that always happened when Shane had a date with her sister. No matter how she tried leaving early and getting to her sister on time, something always cropped up. This time, it was the sobbing bride from the Brightman party.

She parked her car and hurried into their favorite little diner. Without waiting for the hostess, Shane made her way over to their usual table and kissed her sister's cheek.

Francine squealed. "Damn it woman!" she exclaimed. "You almost gave me a heart attack."

Shane grinned as Francine stood to get a hug. Once they were seated, the waitress arrived to take her drink order then leave again.

"You do know I carry a gun?"

Shane merely laughed and gave her another kiss. "Sorry I'm late. But a bride just had to put her foot down to her feuding mother and mother in law and she is not holding up well."

"Yeah." Francine nodded. "That's always hard. So, how are you?"

"Tired—frazzled."

Francine tilted her head. "Why frazzled?"

"I think I've destroyed…" The waitress returned and after she left, Shane continued. "Destroyed what I have with Falcon."

"Child, please. You couldn't do that if you tried."

Shane took a long drink from her cool glass and shrugged. "The other night he came over with Danielle. We were celebrating her getting on the rugby team at school. We talked about the pictures and I thought we cleared the air but I fell asleep during our movie and he went and slept on the couch."

"Dang."

"Right! And the sofa isn't a comfortable

sleep for his large frame."

Francine gave a helpless shrug. "I know he always sleeps beside you when Danielle is over. Do you really think it's because he doesn't want to be around you anymore—because of the pictures? That would be bullshit."

"I don't know what to think. I could just be overreacting. Maybe I was snoring so loud that he couldn't sleep and he just didn't want to embarrass me or something like that."

Francine giggled. "Right. That wouldn't be something Falcon would hide from you. If anything he'd use it to make you blush and drive you crazy."

"True." Shane sighed. "I don't know, sis."

"Maybe he was remembering you in those stunning shots and he got turned on."

Shane was in the process of swallowing another mouthful of juice when her sister blurted that out. She choked sending juice flying through the air. Francine leaned to the side to avoid getting splattered. "Why would you go and say something like that?" She asked around bouts of coughing. "Jesus! What is wrong with you and Jana!"

Francine frowned. "Would you prefer him find you disgusting?"

"Of course not! But it's Falcon we're talking about here. There's no way seeing me in those pictures did anything like that to him. The man's seen me in my bra and panties and hadn't gotten turned on."

"Yes, but you have to remember, some men could see you naked and not feel anything. But to see you sexual drives them mad."

"What's the difference?"

"Um...Okay, let's look at it another way." Francine leaned back in her chair, shifted easily to the side and tossed her right arm over the back of it. "If—hypothetically speaking—if Falcon was to come to you and say *I want to be more than friends,* what would you say?"

"After asking him if he'd been drinking?"

"Seriously?"

Shane rolled her shoulders. "Falcon is a good man. He's trustworthy, kind, loyal…"

"All the things we said we wanted in a future husband. So what's the problem?"

"The problem is none of the women he's dated looks anything like me. And I'm not going to say he's vain, it just—never came up I guess."

"Do you want Falcon?"

"As in…" Shane glanced over her shoulders before leaning in. "As in…sexually?"

"How else do you think I mean?"

Shane thought about it. She rested against the back of her chair and really, truly pondered the question. Falcon was a good looking man, the kind of man who could grace the cover of any romance novel. He had a job, a respectable one and he loves his little girl with everything. She knew the kind of gentle soul he was and, Francine was right, he had all the qualities she wrote down when they were little girls and were planning their weddings. "I guess I would have to switch my way of thinking about him. He's been my friend for so long—why am I even thinking about this anyway?"

"Well, because he left you alone in bed and you feel as if he's cheating."

Shane eyed her sister. "Why would you even say that? That's a dumb thing to say."

"Is it? Sweetie, you've tried the rest. Right? Why not try Falcon? If all fails you go back to being friends."

"Or it could blow up in my face."

Francine giggled.

"Seriously! That's where your mind went?"

"Where did my mind go?"

Shane opened her mouth to speak but the waitress returned with their meals. She clamped her mouth shut and waited until their server left before continuing. "Forget it. All I'm saying is if I reevaluate how I feel about Falcon and he doesn't even want to consider a new level to our relationship it'd kill me."

"Worse than how you are right now?"

The two ate silently. Shane thought speaking

to her sister would clear things up in her head. Maybe Francine would tell her she was reading too much into Falcon leaving the bed. She figured Francine would tell her that he left the bed because she was snoring or talking in her sleep—something that would make her feel a bit better about the whole situation. Instead, the talk make everything a lot more convoluted.

"Maybe you should just talk to him," Francine said. "Tell him that him leaving you alone made you feel as if he was still upset."

"No. That will only make things worse."

"Okay." Francine tapped the corners of her lips with the cloth napkin. "What are you going to do?"

"Nothing."

Francine rolled her eyes and picked up her napkin to wipe her lips. "How is that working out for you? The saying nothing deal."

"I don't—I just—I want—damn it!"

"That's what I thought." Francine dropped her napkin in her lap.

Shane switched the topic to how her store was doing. That conversation quickly snowballed into another and soon they were far away from the dangerous topic of Falcon James. By the time their date was over and Shane hugged her sister, all she wanted was to go home and take a shower. Still, she stopped by the store and helped Anisa close for the evening. She then dropped her employee home before finally turning her car toward home.

The moment she was in the door, Shane kicked off her shoes, set the alarm, poured herself a glass of wine and climbed into bed with her laptop.

If she started dating again that would put a stop to all her crazy thoughts about Falcon. She was snoring and he left the bed just to get some sleep—that was what she would go with. There could be no other possible explanations. She tapped away at the keyboard to a few different websites before she remembered the one she truly intended on getting to. She just couldn't remember the name.

www.findyourman.com

Francine had used it to find a few dates before. Though nothing panned out, none of the men turned out to be axe-wielding Dexter in training. Though Shane had an account on the site, she never found anyone she was remotely interested in and after living on the site for about a month, she began keeping her distance. From time to time she'd go on, when she could remember the password, and delete all the messages that were clogging up her inbox. This time when she got in, there were only two messages. One from *Chubby_chaser69* and one from *urlastchance.*

"On what fucking planet?" Shane groaned and deleted them without even reading the letters.

She sipped from her wine and set about updating her profile. Still a little iffy about the whole thing, Shane uploaded a picture of herself because all the specs she'd read said she was more likely to get a date if there was a face to go with her name. While in the process, the little bar at the bottom of her screen pinged and glowed green. When she clicked on it, someone with the handle *WhiskeyAlphayankeenovemberecho* popped up. She giggled. "Very clever, Wayne."

The first thing she did was checked his profile. It said *WhiskeyAlphayankeenovemberecho* was ex-military but was now an executive chef. The man was gorgeous with crisp blue eyes, dark hair with a hit of grey and strong cheekbones. With a mental shrug, Shane clicked on the message.

"Hi there. I see you're online."

"Yes. How are you?" Shane typed back.

"Tired. It was a long day. How are you?"

Shane gave a one shoulder shrug, trying to find the right way to answer that simple question. *"I'm okay. Spent some time with my sister."*

"Do you require bail? Lol!"

"Lol. *No. My sister and I aren't like that which*

is weird to most people." She responded.

"That's amazing. My sister and I were always fighting growing up. Didn't have that issue with my brother – strange."

Shane laughed. *"Well, isn't it obvious? You were boys."*

"LOL! Probably. So, anything you want to ask me before I ask you out to dinner?"

Shane's heart hammered in her chest. Could she really go on a date with some strange guy she met online? Sure, he was good looking, muscular, slightly graying hair which she found surprisingly sexy – but did she have it in her?

"Too soon?" WhiskeyAlphayankeenovemberecho asked.

"No. Well, we could try dinner. If I asked you everything now, what would we talk about then?"

"Lol. You got me there. Are you free tomorrow night? I know you own your own business and your time is valuable."

Shane grinned. *"I can be free tomorrow night – around seven."*

"Well, I have a table at Condor's. If you know where that is."

"I certainly do." Shane was impressed. The wait list to get onto the reservation list at Condor's was a year long. Yet this man had his own table there. *"I'm Shane by the way."*

"Shane?"

"Yes. My mother was in love with the Jack Schaefer novel. And yes, I am female."

"There were no doubts about your sex. I've seen your picture."

Shane laughed.

"I'm Wayne."

"I know. My best friend taught me military alphabet."

"Very few people get my name from all that," Wayne wrote. *"I'm glad you did."*

"Okay. I should go. I have a running facetime date with my God daughter but I will see you tomorrow night at 7."

"It was good speaking with you, Shane."

Once she read that, Shane logged out. She set

the computer aside and tried catching her breath. This was her chance to see if she could really survive the dating world.

The days Falcon took to do reports and other admin duties of the Captain, were often times the worse. He hated sitting behind a desk, staring at a computer screen for prolonged periods of time. To make matters worse, he'd woken up with a migraine that didn't seem to want to go away.

With a frown, he tapped away at his keyboard, entering information and rechecking accounts of arrests from the week before.

Most of the reports were already done but after each arrest and the team submitted their reports, it was his job to go through them and see if there was any red flags. Each member had to give their account from their position and point of view. It was a way for the department to cover their asses if anything cropped up—like a lawsuit. It was a boring and laborious gig.

Honestly, he'd rather be busting down doors and tackling perpetrators any day but with any promotion came more work and most of it becomes administrative and mundane.

When Shane stuck her head into his office, he couldn't suppress the smile he felt on his face.

"Knock. Knock!" sShe said.

"Shane!" Falcon walked around his desk to hug her. "I didn't know you were coming. Did I forget a lunch date or something?"

"Nope. Can't a girl just pop in to visit her best friend in the entire world?"

Falcon laughed. "Oh boy."

"It's nothing bad, I promise." Shane said. "I wanted to surprise you and since I know you very well, I know you haven't eaten all day." She held up a brown paper bag with a Phoenix on the side. "I come bearing gifts."

He smiled. "Thanks." Falcon accepted the bag and sat on the edge of his desk. He was busy looking in even as he spoke again. "Listen, a friend of mine had some tickets to the Bravos game tonight. He can't go so he gave them to me. I'm taking the kidlet and I have an extra ticket. Wanna come?"

"Sorry, no can do."

"You're giving up a Bravos game?"

Shane laughed. "For the first time in years, I know. But I have a date."

It was a good thing Falcon was seated and didn't have anything in his mouth. He would have fallen over while choking. "A date?"

"I know, right? A while back I signed up for *findyourman.* I haven't really used the account but last night I decided to log in and delete old messages. He messaged me. We talked and he asked me to dinner—I said yes."

"You're going out with a complete stranger?"

"Yeah. The men I know want nothing to do with me. I'm tired of being alone, Falcon. The men in my life want to be friends but none of them is remotely interested in anything else. I'm nobody's type. Sure, this won't turn into my happily ever after but this is my first date in two years and I'm going."

"At least tell me his name so I can check him out."

"No!" Shane frowned. "What *is* the matter with you?"

"Nothing. You just want to know what you're walking into!" Falcon returned. "I thought you'd want that."

"This isn't one of your *operations,* Falcon. I told you because you're my friend and I thought you'd be happy for me. But don't mistake that for me asking you for permission."

Falcon frowned. It seemed each time he opened his mouth he was just making things worse. He didn't mean to sound like a jealous idiot. The thought of her going out with another man sent something surging through his veins then gripping his stomach like fingers contracting. It all left him feeling sick and crazy. "Of course I know you don't need my permission!" Falcon said a little angrier than he meant to. "But this is some chump from a website!"

"Don't call him that—you don't know him."

"And neither do you!"

"Low blow coming from you, Falcon."

Falcon took a deep breath, a sanity restoring breath and nodded. "Fine. But do this date thing somewhere public, somewhere..."

Shane grabbed her purse and glared at him. "I can have my date where ever I want—in the middle of Times Square or in his bed. You're not my father. You're supposed to have my back and be happy for me but instead you're acting like a jackass!"

"Shane!"

"No. Leave me alone!" She stormed from his office and Falcon darted after her.

He wasn't sure when she'd learn to walk that fast in heels but before he managed to reach the end of the hall she was gone. Though Falcon wanted to punch someone or something, he settled for biting the back of his right index finger.

Well, I definitely didn't handle that well.

"That was the stupidest argument I've ever been a part of." Falcon muttered to himself. "The absolute, dumbest load of…" He turned to head back inside and almost knocked Topaz over coming through the door.

"Hey!" Topaz shouted. "Cool it."

Falcon sucked his teeth.

"What's with all the yelling?"Topaz asked

Falcon rubbed the back of his neck before turning to look at Topaz. "Shane is going on a date tonight. I didn't handle it well."

"Jealous idiot?"

Falcon's first instinct was to deny but he knew Topaz. His friend would see right through him, they'd get into an argument and Falcon would come off looking like the jackass. Instead, he decided to bypass all that with a nod. "Yup. Jealous idiot. I don't know. When she told me I panicked and then I just got a bad feeling about it." He headed back toward his office.

"Bad feeling as in, you want to run this guy over with your car for even looking at Shane cross-eyed or bad feeling something isn't right?"

Falcon said nothing.

"Dude, seriously?" They made it to the office and Topaz leaned his back into the wall by the window. "You can keep denying it all you want but we both know that woman has turned something on inside you and you can't switch it off. Instead of fighting it like a beast, you might want to face it. If not, you're going to lose her and we both know you don't want that."

"What am I supposed to say, huh?" Falcon dragged his fingers through his hair. "It's not like I can just call her up and tell her not to go out with this guy, to go out with me instead. Shane is not that kind of woman. And if I ruin this for her she'd never forgive me."

Topaz sighed. "You're damned if you do, damned if you don't."

Falcon stood beside his friend, folded his arms and stared out the window at the highway behind the station. Cars buzzed back and forth making him feel trapped for he wasn't free to come and go as they were. "And in the mean time she's going out with another man. Before those damn pictures I didn't have a reason to see her as more than my friend. I would have happily given her advice. I was content with that, happy with that, but then to find out she has those curves, that perfectly cool chocolate of her flesh in some of the most intimate areas of her body—Paz, how am I going to pretend I'm not pissed off knowing another man gets to see all that and everything else?"

"Well, there are no guarantees it'll go well." Topaz patted Falcon's shoulder. "It could suck."

"Then she'll be miserable. I don't want that either."

"Well, shit, brother! I don't know!"

"Yeah. Wanting her isn't enough. If she can find happiness with another man then I won't stand in the way of that. She deserves the best of everything. Even though I know all that and I believe it with all my heart, that knowledge doesn't make it suck any less."

"Are you sure this isn't one of those *if I can't have her no one else can* situations?"

"Would you stop being a dick?" Falcon said. "I know what I'm feeling, all right?"

"All right." Topaz held up his hands in surrender. "Sheesh. Keep your draws on. I just—I had to ask."

Falcon nodded.

"You're going to need to figure this shit out. You're driving me crazy and I have to depend on you to watch my back."

"You know I'd never let you down."

"Not intentionally." Topaz headed for the door but stopped. "Fix this, Falcon."

Falcon nodded and Topaz exited the office.

"Fix it." Falcon muttered. "How do I do that without making this explode?"

That question remained a part of him for the rest of the day. By the time he was leaving the office, he hadn't even touched the food Shane had brought him. Instead, he binged on coffee and cookies from the break room and dropped Shane's delivery into the nearby garbage can on his way out the front door.

Barely at his front door, his phone started ringing. He grabbed it instantly for he thought it was Shane but it turned out to be Topaz. Probably checking on him after the conversation they had earlier in the day about his reaction to Shane dating. "Yeah, brother."

"You have to come back to the house," Topaz said. "Marshals need our help with something."

"How much time?"

"As soon as you can get here."

"Okay, on my way."

He flipped a u-turn and raced toward the station again. After placing a call to let Danielle.

"So we're missing the game?" Danielle asked.

"Well, I am. The tickets are in my office on top of the laptop. You can take Charlie."

Danielle sighed dramatically. "Fine. Can I take some money from the stash?"

"Sure," Falcon said. "I love you."

"Love you too—and dad?"

"Yeah, sweetie?"

"Be careful, would you?"

"I promise."

After hanging up, Falcon slipped his siren on to bypass traffic. The moment he was in through the doors, Topaz and another member of his team, Dawson Mullings fell into step beside him.

"The Marshals are on their way," Topaz said. "But they've been trying to get a hold of this guy for a while now and they won't make it here in time. They want to know if we could pick him up. Upstairs said we would give them a hand."

Falcon took the picture Dawson offered and stared into the blue eyes of the perp they'd be going after.

"His rap-sheet is really long," Dawson said. "It started all the way back to the late eighties with burglary. Then he seemed to graduate to armed robbery, evading, then he tossed in a little more burglary for old times' sake while adding uttering terroristic threats…"

"The armed robbery—gun?"

"Yeah."

"What else is on that sheet?"

"Attempted murder—charges were dropped after their only witness turned up missing."

"Missing my ass." Falcon frowned.

Topaz spoke up. "There is a patrol car sitting on the location."

"Okay. Paz, try getting eyes inside. We need to know about possible casualties and collateral damages. Dawson, have Belle find us floor plans. We may have to go in quiet."

"Got it, Cap'n," Dawson said.

"Let me gear up. Gather the crew in the boardroom."

The two men beside him nodded and turned back the other way. He quickly found his locker and changed. Once he was in the large meeting room with his crew, he read over the report from the marshals then passed out the Fact Sheet on their newest mission.

"Okay," Falcon said. "Show me what you got."

"The floor plan is pretty sketchy," Belle Jackson explained, pointing to her computer screen. "There is only one place I can be to get a good shot if the perp's inside the building when I'm needed. These are the latest plan since the last reno. It's not very detailed."

Falcon frowned.

"Um…boss?" Dawson hollered from behind them. "You may want to take a look at this."

"Find us an entry, Belle." Falcon hurried to hunch over Topaz's shoulder. "What's up?"

But Topaz didn't have to speak. He merely pointed to the screen and Falcon's heart fell from his chest to the ground. There, in the flesh, sitting across from the very man they were after, was Shane Teller.

A sharp pain pulsed behind Falcon's right

eye.

"She couldn't have picked someone else?" Dawson asked. "*Anyone* else?"

"Shit!" Falcon muttered.

"I guess that bad feeling you had was right," Topaz said. "Now, if you want to sit this one out…"

"No." Falcon ground his teeth as he thought. Instantly, he began working through plots in his head. He focused on the blueprint for the restaurant. They could do an entry through the skylight but that would draw way too much attention. If Wayne was armed, Falcon could get hurt.

Going through the front door was out of the question because there were too many people seated around Shane's table.

The best bet was to make entry by way of the kitchen then come out through the door that was directly across from the perp's table. He relayed that to his team with one added warning. "If he's riled up, put him down. But do not, I repeat, *do not*, shoot Shane."

This mission was unlike any they'd ever been on. Falcon knew that. This time he had something to lose and he hated that sensation. Maybe if he'd put his foot down harder, insisted she tell him who this fool had been—then again she'd hate him for that.

Shit, she already hates you.

Falcon ran a gloved hand over the back of his helmet covered head. Topaz had been right when he said no matter what, Falcon could never win.

It took less than twenty minutes to reach Condor's. The men and woman in the back were silent as they always were on their way to bust through a door. It was their solitude that calmed themselves. The truck slowed and Falcon got a better grip on the M4 Carbine he carried and cleared his throat.

"All right people," Falcon said as he usually did. "Anyone gets shot tonight buy the drinks."

The crew chuckled.

"Seriously, watch your brother's and sister's six." He stressed.

The vehicle stopped, Falcon pushed opened the door and Belle alighted and disappeared in the darkness. Since Belle was their sniper, she had to get settled before they made a move.

The rest waited in silence.

"In position." Her voice was strong through his headset. "Whenever you boys are ready we can get the show on the road."

Under the cover of darkness they made their way in through the back and quickly, silently and evacuated the kitchen staff. With the patrol officers watching over those, the team continued on their way. Falcon and Dawson were the first through the door. The rest of the team took up positions, blocking the other patrons from the perp with their bodies and weapons.

"Hello Christopher," Falcon said, training his weapon on the perp.

"Falcon! What are you doing?" Shane demanded. "You can't use resources like this to ruin my date!"

Falcon frowned. He carefully pulled the picture from his pocket and dropped it on the table before her. "Don't flatter yourself." He growled. "Now, stand up slowly and move away from the table.

"Falcon..."

"Not a request, Shane."

She gathered her purse and the picture and was moving toward Topaz when Christopher reached for her. Shane slammed a fist into his throat then in the back of the head. When Christopher landed face first on the table, Shane shifted behind Topaz. Once she was out of harm's way, Falcon motioned for Dawson to step forward. Christopher Wayne was quickly handcuffed.

"Target secure," Falcon said to Belle through the mouthpiece.

While Topaz and Dawson walked their collar out to the waiting van, Falcon lowered his gun and approached Shane who was still staring down at the mug shot, hands shaking. "Are you all right?"

"I-I think so."

"Good. Do you want a ride home?"

"No—no I brought my car."

Falcon wished he could hold her, to kiss her hands to stop them from shaking or make love to her to make them shake for a whole other reason. But he was *numero uno* on her list of people she detested in that moment. "Okay."

With a final glance, Falcon headed out the door. Crowding Shane would do no good at that moment; especially since he hadn't been sure what she thought of him anymore.

The van with the Christopher was already on it's way to lock up and his team were hanging around, waiting for him. Though none of them said anything, Belle and Topaz patted his shoulder before they piled back into the transport.

CHAPTER FOUR

The night after the raid on Condor's, Shane couldn't face the world. The media kept calling her house, asking her to comment on the videos making their way around the internet, swiftly sailing to viral status. They wanted to know if she knew anything about Wayne's criminal history, if she was involved with any of his crimes, if she wanted to comment on what the tabloids were calling *a night of binging with a serial killer.*

It seemed every jack-off with a camera thinks they're some kind of professional or something. One of the bottom feeders had sold their video to the highest bidder, and now Shane was the town's top story.

Shane hid. What she really wanted to do was

tell them all to eat shit and die. But she knew the media very well. That would only make things worse, draw attention to her sister and the store.

After a few hours of that kind of torture, she fought through the photographers hounding her front lawn and climbed behind the wheel of her car. A few of them stepped in front of her car to shoot off a few more pictures and Shane slammed her foot on the gas. They yelped and drove out of the way.

Enough is fucking enough.

She wandered around the city, desperately trying to find a place to get lost. Usually, she'd go to Falcon and he'd accept her with open arms and a bowl of Neapolitan ice-cream. But how could she face him when she'd make such a colossal mess of things? In the end, Shane wound up where she would go after Falcon—Francine's house. Though the media found her there, Francine used her connection as a police detective and a few phone calls later, a group of squad cars showed up and the rag tag bunch of bottom feeders dispersed.

Day one of was finally over and that night as Francine pulled the sheets up to her shoulders and kissed her head, Shane burst into tears. All through the next day she wept softly in the room alone. She didn't understand how she hadn't run dry yet. Every time she thought of the things she's said to Falcon, the way she felt when his team burst through that kitchen door and the coldness in his eyes during—all of it made her sob even more.

From time to time Francine would come in and brought in food, after a while of her just ignoring it, Francine showed up with fruits. Shane picked at the grapes, ate all the pineapple pieces and curled herself back into a ball.

"Shane?" Francine called.

Her footsteps were light against the hardwood floor. Shane didn't move. She only closed her eyes tighter and held her breath. Maybe if she pretended she was dead, Francine would go away.

"Shane…I brought you something to eat."

"I'm not hungry."

"I don't care," Francine said. "Eat it. Seriously, Shane. I know this date thing ended in disaster but you can't stay in this bed forever. You can't stay with me forever. And one day, maybe not today because I'm telling you to do it, but one day, you're going to have to face Falcon again."

"So he can tell me *I told you so?*"

"You're being childish!" Francine snapped. "Fine. Okay? Shit didn't work out like you planned. So what? You're going to have to get off your ass and face reality. Falcon didn't do anything wrong. I would have done the same thing if you told me about this date. He was trying to protect you and still you acted like a spoiled teenager. Get your ass up and eat!"

Shane rolled over. All she wanted to do was tell Francine to go kill herself but the last time she allowed anger to drive her, she wound up on a date with a bank robber who tried to kill a cop.

"I'm sorry. I just—after so many years of not having a guy take a second look I was happy he did. It was too good to be true and Falcon saw it."

"That's not what Falcon saw." Francine unfolded her arms and sat on the side of the bed. She picked up a mug from where it was sitting on the chair on a tray and handed it to Shane. "He's a cop. He might have felt something was wrong but he's no mind reader. Look, Falcon is the one friend who's had your back since you were a kid. He's never once hurt you, has he? Fix this, Shane. If you don't you will lose him and that beautiful God daughter of yours."

"How can I face him after this? Especially with the things I said to him, the way I said them, how can I possibly look him in the eyes now?"

Francine chuckled. "Very bravely. Sis, friends fight, all the time. What determines the strength of said friendship is how you make up—if you make up."

Shane sighed.

"You're strong, Shane. Walk in like *I run this bitch!*"

"Oi." Shane laughed. She sipped from the coffee and moaned.

"I'm serious." Francine stressed. "Even if you don't feel that strength, fake it until you do. Men like women who are strong."

"No they don't."

"I didn't say little boys, Shane. I said men and Falcon is a fine-ass, grown-ass *man* even if you don't want to admit it."

Shane didn't want to think of Falcon's ass. Well, maybe just a little bit. She allowed herself a few seconds to remember the way it looked moving away from her decked out in good-guy dark blue then down to the gun holsters strapped tightly around his large, muscular thighs.

"Shane? Sweetie?" Francine snapped her fingers before Shane's eyes. "You still with me?"

"Um…" Shane glanced around quickly then

smiled. "Yeah. Well, I better get to it then."

"*After* you eat."

Shane made a face. Still, to appease her sister, she picked up a half of the grilled cheese sandwich and took a bite. Her stomach wasn't happy she'd decided to put anything but water in her mouth. Still, she managed to eat most of the food on the plate then smiled at her sister. "Better?"

"Much. Now, go get your man."

"He's not my man."

"Yeah, yeah. Whatever. Go talk to Falcon."

Shane dragged out getting dressed and driving over to Falcon's. If she called him first, there was a chance he would be screening his calls. So, Shane spent a good portion of the time hunting him down. From the station, to his gym, to the gun range—finally she drove to his house and parked on the curb. His truck wasn't in the driveway but she waited. After about two hours, and her napping for a portion of it, the sound of his truck pulled around her car and into the driveway. Danielle was the one driving, she could tell for there was some heavy maneuvering for the vehicle to be straight. When the door finally opened and Falcon hopped from the passenger side, he stalked immediately to her car. She stepped out.

"Hi." Her voice was small and trembling.

"Godie!" Danielle called. "Did you see that? Am I good or what?"

Shane spared Danielle a grin. "I'm very proud of you." The two hugged.

"Can I talk to your dad alone for a second?"

"Are you two going to fight again?" Danielle asked. "I know you've been having issues because he's been a pain in the…"

"Danielle. Claudia. James." Falcon's voice held a warning.

"Going!" Danielle said.

She waved at Shane and darted into the house. Shane inhaled deeply, held the breath before resting her elbow on the room of the car just above the driver's door.

"I'm sorry," Shane said. "I didn't mean to come off like such a desperate idiot."

Falcon said nothing. His silver eyes dazzled at her with an unreadable expression she'd never seen before in Falcon's gaze. "I just wanted you to be happy for me."

"I was—happy for you, Shane. You have a right to date whoever you want and I shouldn't have said anything."

"Even though you were right?"

"I take no pleasure in that." Falcon turned for the front steps and Shane followed. "I just wanted you to be safe. I—I wanted—you could have gotten hurt. When the guys showed me the footage from the restaurant and I saw you sitting across from him, I swear, I died inside."

"I'm sorry."

"Don't say that." Falcon picked at the corner of his right thumb before looking over at her again. "I knew, deep down that when we bust in there, things could have gone down badly."

"But they didn't. You saved me."

"That's not—" Falcon sighed. "There's no winning in this situation.

They sat together on the top step, so close, Shane could feel the heat radiating from Falcon's body even though they weren't touching. Usually when they sat there, he would bounce her gently with his shoulder until she laughed. Then she would lean her head to his shoulder and sighed with the thought this man would do anything for her. This man was her friend.

Shane held her breath, waiting for it to come, but Falcon didn't move—she didn't even think he was breathing.

Shane wondered what was going on inside Falcon's head but she didn't speak. The wind whistled through the leaves of the large oak trees around the house. From somewhere in the distance, the sound of sirens followed by heavy engines raced along the road. A dog barked then whimpered to their left and a lone car chugged up the street by Falcon's house. The pulse of music filled the air from behind them—Danielle was playing her stereo.

"I wanted to kill him." Falcon said, his voice harsh and jarring through her peace. "I saw him with you and I wanted him dead."

"I shouldn't have gone out with him. Not so soon. I should've known better."

"You're an adult, Shane. Adults date. You can't live your life not interacting with people because I think they're shady. It's really up to you."

Shane cleared her throat.

Silence, except for the sound of Danielle's stereo and not long that was gone too. Even the trees stopped whistling. Shane watched the road, maybe looking for tumbleweeds to go by. For the first time in their friendship

"Why did you act that way?" Shane asked, turning to stare at Falcon. His he tightened his jaw but didn't turn his attention to her. "I'm just curious. Franny said when cops get a certain feeling, they know something is wrong."

"I'm not psychic."

"That's not what I'm saying..."

He looked at her then and Shane's heart almost stopped. Even though she wanted to turn away, the intense heat in his gaze kept her sweetly captive. Slowly, Falcon inched closer.

Of course it was all in her head! It had to be in her head!

Even if he had moved the action was purely to shake some sense into Shane and nothing more. Falcon had never once shown any interest in her aside from being a friend, a confidant to him and his daughter. Shane had to have been mistaking what she read in that moment, the heat that radiated from his stare to caress her like a feather.

There was no way Falcon would want to kiss her...Shane's eyes drifted close for though she tried, she couldn't control her actions anymore.

Then their lips met and sparks flew inside Shane's head. Every alarm that could possible sound inside her went off. Yet when she lifted her arms to his chest with every intention of pushing him away, her fingers betrayed her and curled into his shirt, pulling him closer. Her eyes drifted closed and the kiss spun out of control. Her body shook, she pulsed between her legs and every hair on her body stood on end. Everything about that moment, his scent, the roughness of his day old stubble against her skin, the lush, fullness of his lips—all of it aroused her into a kind of frantic desperation.

Falcon was her best friend. Having him be intimate with her shouldn't make her want to fly. Yet, there she was, giving him access to her tongue, her mouth, her whole soul. There she was, sitting on his porch, returning his affections with the same ferocity.

Though he plundered her mouth with his tongue, drawing from her moans and gasps, Falcon never once touched her. He braced one arm against the step and the other laid across his lap.

She released his shirt with one hand and cradled the side of his face gently and Falcon seemed to take that as the permission he needed to deepen the kiss. A soft moaned escaped her body, jarring her back to reality and she somehow found the strength to push away from him.

"Damn." Shane whispered.

"Mmm," Falcon replied.

"What—um—what was that—"

"I probably should've warned you about that..." Falcon's voice cracked. "I should've..."

Shane got up and hurried down the steps.

"You can't be running away from this!" Falcon called.

"No. Not running. I need to put some space between you and me right now. I need to clear my head. There is no way that can happen if your body is within arms' reach."

"I could apologize."

She stopped and faced him over the roof of her car. "Would you mean it?"

"No." Falcon shook his head.

"Then why offer?"

"It'd make you feel better." Falcon tossed his hands up. "It would take away the blame on your part since you kissed me back."

"There's no blame, Falcon. We kissed."

Falcon gave her a one shoulder shrug. "I know. I was there."

"Falcon..."

"Go, take your space. We can talk about it later."

"I'm not running." Shane stressed. "I promise."

"I know, Shane."

"Um...It's only for a little while." She rested her arms on top of the car and picked at the corners of her fingers silently. "Birdman?"

"Yeah?"

Shane took a labored breath and wrapped her arms self-consciously around herself. "Could you—um—could you come over tomorrow night?"

"Why?"

"I would like to see you."

Falcon smiled, that one that made the corners of his eyes crinkled showing how much he'd laughed in his life. It was the one that pulled his lips upward at the sides, showing how perfect his teeth were. It was the same show of mirth that Shane found herself being drawn to more and more in the past few days. "I-I don't mean to be vague or weird. Could you..."

"You know you don't need an excuse to see Danielle." Falcon rested his hands to his hips. "You just have to call."

"No—not with Danielle. I—uh—I want you—to—um—come—alone."

"Okay. Sure, Shane. I'll come over."

Shyness filled her then and her eyes instantly fell to her toes as she laughed softly. "See you tomorrow then."

"Okay."

Shane threw her body into the driver's seat and after starting the engine, she peeled from the curb without putting seatbelt on. She was halfway home before she remembered to. Still, she couldn't help feeling a lovely warmth in her core that threatened to overwhelm her. Falcon James had kissed her. He'd tasted from her mouth, made her wet and as he looked at her with those beautiful eyes, as she began seeing him more as a lover than a friend, he had stood firm behind his actions. Some men would apologize and run away but not Falcon.

He'd made her moan without laying a finger on her body. Falcon proved what she'd feared, that he knew precisely what to do to his woman to make her go mindless and still beg for more. He'd tasted her and given her so much in that one kiss, Shane was confused. But one thing she knew for certain, it drove her crazy in all the best ways that he wasn't in the least bit sorry for what he'd done to her.

"Woohoo!" Shane fist pumped.

Chapter Five

What the hell was I thinking?

It hadn't been planned. But over the years, they'd automatically fallen into the friend zone. There wasn't even a chance for either of them to think of the other as more. Being his friend came naturally to her. And with being his friends, he'd always come to her about women, asking her thoughts. Whenever he had a breakup, she always had a hug and a cold beer ready for him as well as an available ear. In those moments, Shane was contented to be his buddy. Now that she tasted his kiss, felt those beautiful lips pressed into her and experienced that warmth throbbing within her core, Shane knew there was no going back. There was no washing the feel of his wonderful lips and skillful tongue from her mind. Though she was very certain she'd be ashamed for it later, Shane could also imagine that tongue between her legs—from lashing the tender spots behind her knees, then up her thighs to…

Honk!

Shane screamed and gripped the wheel. When she finally realized what was happening, she frowned. It seemed she'd come to the stoplight and while waiting had drifted off to lala land. And although it was her fault for not paying attention, she was tempted to give the driver behind her the finger. Shane refrained, put on her right signal and turned.

She slowed to see if there were any media still lurking by her place. When she saw no one, Shane figured they were off hounding someone else. Thankful she could go back to some semblance of normalcy in her life, she pulled the Wraith into the driveway, pressed the garage button on her visor and stopped as the door lifted. It took a few seconds before it was high enough for her to ease the car in. She pressed the button again and the door closed, plunging the room into darkness until the automatic lights flickered on. Once they did, she exited the car, grabbed her purse and let herself out the side door then in through the front.

Shane closed the front door and pressed her back against it. Slowly, she slid to the floor feeling light headed. Covering her face with her hands, Shane inhaled deeply, held the breath, counted to ten inside her head, then exhaled through her mouth. That did nothing to help—in fact, the action caused a dull pulse to develop behind her right eye. It twitched a few times before going back to a slow throb. Her hands shook slightly, her head throbbed and no matter how hard she tried, Shane couldn't stop her body from trembling.

Coming down from an adrenaline high was a bitch.

For a silent eternity, Shane remained where she was, legs now stretched out before her and apart. The thoughts inside her head went from darkness, to fear to confusion. Her mind and body did battle for what was to come of the debacle between herself and Falcon. In the end, her body won and Shane couldn't stop herself from tailing her right hand down the left side of her neck, over her shoulder then down her arm. She pressed her eyes closed and allowed thoughts of Falcon to swim unobstructed through her mind.

It started with his smile, to the way his cheeks indented with those dimples until finally, him walking toward her shirtless with his hoodie in one hand. Shane licked her lips, arched into the door and slipped her right hand over her breast, stopping only to pinch at her nipple. A soft, feeble whimper left her lips and she dropped her hand further. Between her legs, she used two fingers to press against the tender jewel there after bring her legs up to plant the soles of her feet against the floor. The wetness from beneath the soft, lacy fabric was more than evident, it soaked through the material and slid against her finger. Biting her lower lip, she stroked up and down, loving the friction against her for it sent charges of electricity surging up her spin then down again to curl her toes.

"Falcon." She whispered, pressing harder.

He came to her in that moment, tall and handsome with grey eyes dancing mischievously at her. Everything from his hard chest with the rich darkness of his nipples to the way he walked into a room made her pulse soaking her panties more. There was a strength in Falcon, in the way he does everything that was such a turn on. She trailed her free hand against the inside of one thigh, then the next even as her hand continued circular patterns against her wetness.

The taste of his kiss was unlike anything she'd ever experienced. No man had managed to make her melt just by pressing their lips together. Shane never thought that was possible – to have a man give her so much in such a short time. His scent came back to her then and though she didn't recognize the cologne, she had every intention of finding out what it was and buying him a bottle just so he could keep using it. He'd moaned for her, showed weakness and strength in that one sound. Hearing he was caught up in the emotion as much as she was weakened her body even more.

Soon stroking herself through the confines of her panties hadn't been enough. She craved bare touch against wet flesh. She slid the seat of her panties aside and rewarded herself with a finger caressing up and down her intimately, against the bud and lower to slide the tip in. Shane gasped, pressed her free hand into the floor and gyrate her hips upward. That moment sent her finger deeper, past the first knuckle before she trembled and pulled back. She continued like that, teasing herself, imagining Falcon was there before her, touching her the way she liked to be touched and showing her new ways to make herself scream. Her breathing became strangled as she tried keeping her sounds of pleasure in. She failed miserably when her finger was replaced by Falcon's tongue.

Shane rode her finger hard, bracing her shoulders against the door, holding onto the floor with her free hand and slamming her hips forward, taking her whole finger. She trembled, whimpered and when the need inside became so great, Shane did something she'd never done before—she screamed for Falcon, begged him, pleaded with him. The pressure inside her grew greater and greater. The world around her became invisible—nothing could break through the haze inside her head.

Using her thumb to rub her tender bud, Shane shoved her hips forward one final time and the world around her shattered. Her legs trembled violent and she crashed into the floor, back arched, mouth opened in a silent scream. She gushed against her hand and dripped down her legs and all she could do in the end was let the floor hold her, panting for breath and feeling as if she'd done the worse thing in the world.

Yet, Shane couldn't get past the aftershocks of her orgasm, the weakness in her limbs and the blissful aftermath of all those beautiful sparks of flames charging through her blood. She remained on the floor, legs askew like a doll forgotten. No matter how badly she should feel for what she'd done, Shane couldn't get rid of the smile on her lips and the beautiful pulse that remained between her thighs. She stayed on the floor, staring straight ahead.

After an eternity, she managed to gather herself enough to pull her clothes back together and grab the mop and bucket from the storage room. She cleaned the hardwood floor, trying to remember the last time her climax was so hard—it never had been. Falcon did that—thoughts of him pulled something loose inside her.

With that task finished, Shane took a shower and left the house. She knew touching herself to thoughts of her best friend couldn't happen again and knew if she stayed home it would.

Instead, she marched right on down to her store, and put herself to work.

"You weren't due in tonight, boss lady," Anisa said.

"I know."

"Everything okay?"

Shane nodded. "Yeah, everything's fine." She lied. It would do no good telling Anisa the truth. "I was bored at home. I figure I could come in and get some more promotion things done and roam around the website to see if anything else is falling apart on it. The appointment application has been acting up lately so I need to address that—how was your date?"

"It was everything I thought it would be," Anisa replied, spinning around like Julie Andrews on the mountain at the beginning of *The Sound of Music*. "She's intelligent, Shane—so intelligent."

"Good. I'm glad."

"We're going out again on Saturday for breakfast." Anisa confided. "I work here and she has something doing in the evening so it works out."

"You taking her out?"

Anisa shook her head. "Nope. She's taking care of it this time since last time I paid. I don't think that's how it's supposed to go but it makes her happy."

Shane grinned. "Happiness—all that matters at this point."

"Amen, boss lady. Amen to that."

The two set to work rearranging the store then fixing the displays at the front. Once that was through, Anisa ordered some supplies for the store while Shane deal with a walk-in customer. By the time it was the end of the day Shane was exhausted and was pretty sure she wouldn't have the energy to think much less anything else so going home would be harmless.

While Danielle sat at the counter doing her homework, Falcon tried his best to be present.

She'd ask him questions from time to time. Most often, he knew the answers and answered right away. Other times he had to get here to repeat herself. After a while Danielle seemed to become irritated with having to repeat herself and set to work silently. He'd spent the whole day wondering what in the world he'd been thinking kissing Shane like that. Then again she could have pushed away, slapped him, voiced her displeasure but instead she took off only to stop and invite him over. That confused him greatly.

But, there was no way for him to feel apologetic about the smooch. Feeling her hand tangled in his shirt, then her palm tender against his cheek while their lips locked was heaven. How could he go back to seeing her as just a friend after that?

"Elle, I'm going out a little later—going to see Shane."

"Is she okay?" Danielle asked. "I know you had to arrest her date."

"How'd you know that?"

"I watch TV, dad," Danielle said in a way that told him he should've known that. "Plus, it's all over the internet. I wanted to ask before but I didn't think you guys were ready to explain all of that. Especially since you've been in a bad mood lately."

"I have?"

"Yeah." She closed her books and stacked them on top of each other.

"My visit tonight has something to do with that," Falcon said. He was omitting the fact she could be calling him over to tell him off. He omitted the fact that he kissed Shane and enjoyed it thoroughly—that he'd been turned on by her, hard as a rock and wanted more. "We just need to clear the air, that's all."

"You two aren't breaking up, are you?"

"Breaking up? Sweetie, we weren't dating."

"You know what I mean."

Falcon chewed on his bottom lip. "No. We aren't breaking up. We just need to talk."

"When adult say *we need to talk* the kids

always suffer."

Falcon cursed inside his head but offered his daughter a smile. "I promise, there won't be any suffering. Shane and I just need to figure out a few things – set some boundaries."

"Boundaries? You make it sound like she's your stalker."

"Elle – It's complicated, okay? We're going to have a talk over a couple of drinks. Nothing to be worried about."

"Okay."

The conversation ended there yet for some reason Falcon didn't think Danielle was satisfied with the outcome. She did the dishes while he finished up some paperwork in his office, all the while watching the clock. A little after six, he closed down the computer, changed into a t-shirt and a pair of jeans and grabbed his keys. He found Danielle in her room picking things up off the floor and talking on the phone with Charlie.

"I'm going," he said.

Danielle stopped to hug him. "Hang on a

second, Charlie." She leveled her brown stare on him. "Be nice to Godie."

"What are you talking about? I'm always nice to Godie."

Danielle cocked a hip, rested her hand on it and tilted her head. It was the same look Shane would give him when all she wanted to say was *"really? That's the answer you're going with?"*

Falcon sighed. "I will," Falcon promised. "I'll be back as soon as I can. I love you."

"Love you too."

He left her bedroom and let himself out the house. Shane hadn't called him all day. That added to the apprehensions he was feeling. It was as if Falcon was driving toward his doom at sixty miles an hour. Even with his nerves, he parked behind her Rolls-Royce Wraith in the driveway and jogged up the front steps. Though he had a key to her house, Falcon knocked.

While he waited his heart exploded, the world ended and everything bad swam through his head. By the time he heard the door open,

Falcon's hands were shaking. Then he saw what she was wearing, a light pink dress that hugged her ample breasts, synched under them then flowed over her curves like clouds. It matched her dark skin perfectly. Her hair was pulled back in a pony tail with some left out at the front that was swept to the right side of her face. Dangling earrings sloped from her ears gracefully brushing her shoulders each time she moved her head.

Shane pressed a palm to his chest and kissed his cheek. The connection was too brief. He wanted it to last longer. Still, he remained where he was until she stepped aside.

"Come in. You had a key, right?"

Falcon nodded. "Yeah. Didn't want to assume—you know?" He walked by her and into the house. Then waited for her to lead him to where she would like to have their conversation.

"Hungry?" Shane asked, pouring them both a glass of wine.

"No—had dinner with the kidlet." Falcon

braced his palm to the island and kept his stare on her. Though it was battle to not look down at the way her breasts swelled at the neck of her dress. "Put me out of my misery, Shane. Why am I here?"

"So I can spend time with you," Shane replied. "We haven't really been doing that and I don't want you to think I'm upset or anything."

"You could have told me you weren't mad at my place last night."

"Can we not complicate this?" Shane asked, extending a glass of wine. "Please? We kissed and I'm trying to deal with that. I'm not used to making out with my friends."

Falcon ignored the glass. She set it before him. "Making out? No, trust me, Shane. If we'd made out, you'd know."

She licked her lips and downed the contents of her glass quickly. When she tried pouring herself more, Falcon reached over and took the bottle from her hand.

"No—I need you to be clear during this

conversation. Tell me, what you want."

"I don't know what I want. No, I don't know if I should want what I think I want." Shane stomped her foot and shook her head. "I figured we could talk – maybe have some dinner then see if you'd like desert later?"

Falcon said nothing. He merely stared at her. After a few silent breaths, Shane seemed to whither and dropped her gaze. She nodded her head and cleared her throat.

"I'm sorry. I took that too far." She whispered. "I have some food if you want we can pack some up and you can take it home. That way you don't have to cook tomorrow and since Danielle is with me on Saturday anyway…"

"Shane…"

"What?"

"Breathe."

She eyed him for a silent moment then shook her head, rolled her shoulders and smiled at him. "Sorry. I'm going on…"

Falcon sighed and made his way around the

counter to stand beside her. He folded his arms and pressed his back into the island. "What are we doing here, Shane? Are we really trying to be more because of a few pictures and a kiss?"

"I thought..." Shane cleared her throat. "I thought there was something else here. Was I wrong?"

He caressed her shoulder but let his hand fall to his side after a couple strokes. "All you have to do is say the word and we can back off—I can back off."

"I want to get to know you."

"We've known for our whole lives. What could you possibly not know about me?"

Shane chuckled. "How you like it."

For a moment, Falcon wasn't sure he understood what she was referring to. "Again, I don't want to assume..."

"Do you want to pull my hair and spank me? Do you want to dominate me, hold me down and take it? Are you a rough lover or a gentle lover—or do you fluctuate? Do you like screamers or the women who says nothing at all?"

Falcon laughed. His arousal jerked to life between his legs as his heart slammed inside him. He couldn't help groaning. There was no controlling it. Hearing her voice flow over those questions sent his blood boiling in the best way. "I could…"

Stupid cell phone!

"You should get that," Shane said.

He smiled even as he reached for the phone and pressed it to his ear. "James."

"Sorry to interrupt your date, cap'n," Topaz said. "Your presence is needed."

"I'll be there soon." Falcon hung up. "I'm not running away. I have to take care of something down by the station. Let's put it this way. You want to find out how freaky I am, Shane? Once you agree to this there's no backing out."

She smirked at him, a look he'd never seen on her before and suddenly he was jealous of any man she'd ever given it to—before or after him.

"I don't run."

"Okay. I'm going to give you a mission of your own. Danielle is sleeping over Charlie's tomorrow. His parents will make sure they both get to school for Friday and then she comes home afterward then you have her for Saturday. I want you to be at my place, at eight p.m. Wear your coat—the khaki one—a pair of heels and nothing underneath."

Shane gasped. "I don't think we should have sex yet…"

"There are other ways for pleasure without penetration, Shane," Falcon said, stepping in close to wrap his arms around Shane's hips. "That's not what this is about. Eight p.m. Do not be late."

"What if I am?"

He kissed her roughly then stepped away. "Don't find out."

Chapter Six

After leaving Shane, it took Falcon some time to get his mind into the game. He drove to the station with a very hard problem between his legs. Luckily, the moment they began throwing mission specs at him, it subsided.

He survived the mission. All through it, he kept on task for he knew if he let his mind wander back to Shane there might be no going home for him or one of this teammates. By the time they had everything wrapped up, Falcon figured his crew deserved breakfast, on him. Most of them declined—they had to get home before the kids left for school or the wife slash girlfriend left for work. After figuring out who would take him up on breakfast, Falcon left the station with a plan of where to meet. He hurried home hoping to catch Danielle before she was off to school then to Charlie's. He found her pouring hot water into a tea mug. He waited until she set the kettle down and backed away from the counter before saying anything. Danielle blew at her tea and Falcon smiled.

"Morning."

True to form, she swirled around almost knocking over her mug. "Ugh!"

"Careful!" Falcon rushed forward. "No burns before school."

Danielle grinned. "How was your night? You said you were going to Godie's but you're wearing the same clothes you left in. Date went well?"

"It wasn't a date." Falcon said, he lifted the kettle back to the stand, recovered the sugar container and set it against the wall beside the flour and salt containers. "We had a talk, then the station called."

Danielle sighed dramatically.

"Want me to make you some scrambled

eggs?" Falcon asked, praying that would make her forget their line of conversation.

"I can't believe you made work cut into your time with Shane." Danielle continued as if he hadn't said a word. "You know that's important time?"

He narrowed his eyes at her. "Yes, but catching a bad guy is also important—eggs?"

"Someone else could've led the team—Uncle Paz could do it. He's awesome."

"Yes. I know you think he's Superman and you would be right but I'm the captain so I have to support my crew."

"Shane would make an awesome mom." Danielle pressed on. "Don't you think?"

"Yes. And she will be one day for the guy lucky enough to be the father to her children—scrambled eggs?"

"Why can't that man be you?"

"Because that's not how it works, Elle." Falcon arched a brow. "You know that. Besides, Shane sees me as a friend, nothing more."

"Dad, do you want more? From Shane, I mean."

Falcon fought to hide the shock on his face. He didn't expect the conversation to take such a turn and honestly, he hadn't been remotely prepared for it. "Um—again, not that simple. Eggs or not?"

"Why do you humans have to complicate everything?"

"And…you aren't human?" Falcon asked, resting a hip to the counter and folding his arms.

"No—I'm more than human. I'm fabulous!" Danielle gave him a bright smile, sipped from her tea and headed for the door. "And yes to scrambled eggs."

Falcon stared after her, eyes narrowed and a smile on his lips. He set about making her breakfast, even a chicken sausage and a side of toasted for her.

"Where's yours?" Danielle asked, climbing on a stool.

He set a plate before her then poured her

some juice. "I'm having breakfast with a few of the guys from the squad this morning. I just wanted to come home first so I can see you before you jet off for the weekend."

"Listen, about what we were talking about earlier." Falcon picked at the corners of one of his thumbs for a second before taking a deep breath and meeting her questioning gaze. "Shane and I—you wouldn't be upset about that?"

"Upset? No, why?"

"Well, I know she isn't your mother and you probably don't want anyone to take her place and all…"

"Is that why you haven't dated? Because you think I'd freak out?"

"No."

"Godie, was right. You're a horrible liar."

Falcon pressed his lips into a thin line. "Fine, not entirely. I wasn't ready. But you know, Shane and I have been friends since we were kids."

"Aunt Francine has told me the stories. I've seen the pictures. Dad, don't worry so much about me. You're an adult and adults date. If it just happens to be Godie that would be the icing on the cake."

He kissed her head. "Eat up. I'll change then drop you at school with all your bags."

"Only taking two this time," Danielle said proudly.

Falcon merely groaned and left the room.

Falcon sat on the hood of this truck, waiting for Topaz, Dawson and Belle to show up so they could have an early morning breakfast. The sun was barely peeking out from behind some menacing looking clouds. He inhaled deeply—it was going to rain. Thunder murmured from the distance proving he was wrong. Rain was a beautiful thing but what was coming would be a storm. In that moment he wondered if he should allow Danielle to be at Charlie's for it but shook his head. Charlie's parents never once disappointed him and when Danielle was with them he knew Charlie would take very good care of her. He thought they would make a great couple except the fact Charlie wasn't into girls.

He shifted and rested his back into the windshield, folded his arms behind his head and stared up at the dimly lit sky. Their bust was a bit problematic and Belle was almost shot. He hated those close calls and near misses. They worried him and during drills he always focused on them. Falcon's team was working in concert with another from a county to the east who weren't as trained as Falcon's gang. One of their groups hadn't cleared a room properly and the suspect was lying in wait there.

Falcon lost his temper once everything was under control and grabbed the captain of the other team by the front of the shirt. He shoved him into the nearest vehicle and pulled in close. "The Two Four are a part of my family." He snarled. "If your boys can't do their jobs we can't work with them. I refuse to lose one of my guys because of that."

"Cap'n..." Belle touched Falcon's arm gently. "I'm still standing, right?"

Falcon didn't take his eyes off his captive. "That's not the point. He knows what I mean."

With a quiet understanding passing between both men, Falcon released him and stalked off.

Thunder rumbled pulling him from the memory of what happened mere hours before. This time it was louder and sounded closer. The scent of the impending rain grew stronger and Falcon grew more restless of what he had asked Shane to do. Would she show up as he asked? Maybe not—maybe she would think he was crazy and a pervert and he couldn't say he blamed her. It wasn't like he could talk to Topaz about it—that would embarrass Shane.

"Hey Cap'n!" Belle hollered.

Falcon jerked upward so quickly, he almost fell right off the hood of the truck. He frowned and slid off. "Seriously?"

Belle grinned and wrapped her arms around Topaz's hips. "Sorry. Come, I'm starving."

He followed them inside and they were seated in their usual booth in the tiny diner. The place was empty except for what looked to be a homeless guy a few seats ahead of them, the single waitress, a scruffy looking guy that they could see through the window leading into the kitchen and a couple making out in a further booth. They ordered and while the others slipped into a deep conversation that was punctuated with outbursts of laughter and table slapping, Falcon said nothing.

He leaned back in his seat, sipping on his coffee and playing over into his head his reaction with Shane the night before. Would he have made love to her if the station hadn't called? Yes—definitely. He'd tasted her and each time she stepped close to him, her body giving off the sweetest scent of hot cinnamon, he wanted to tear her clothes off.

"I should get going," Dawson said after a while. "I promised my brother I'd help him move today."

Falcon reached up to bump fists with Dawson then watched him leave.

" Belle, you're a woman, right?" Falcon asked and instantly felt like an idiot.

True to form, Belle pulled the neck of her Rhonda Rousey graphic t-shirt out and peered at her breasts. "Um..." She groped them then looked at Falcon, bright eyed and grinning. "The last time I checked—why?"

Falcon and Topaz laughed.

"Seriously, Falco, you walked into that one." Topaz teased.

"Yeah." Falcon agreed. "Head first. But seriously for a second. If you're trying to seduce a man and he asks you to show up at his place in heels and a trench coat with nothing under it, would you go or would you punch him in the face?"

"Depends..." Belle replied.

"On what?" Topaz and Falcon chorused.

"On a few things.?" Belle asked. "Is the feeling mutual? Do I want this man as much as he wants me – do I believe he wants me? Am I a freak? How big of a freak is he…the possibilities are endless with that question."

Falcon sighed. "But would you do it?"

"Me? Personally?" Belle smirked. "Hell yes. And I have done it. That was the sexiest…most amazing sex I ever had."

"Why? Is our captain planning on getting a little freaky with someone?" Topaz asked.

"Seriously?" Falcon asked trying to hide a smile but failing. "Shane."

"As in, your best friend, God mother to your baby, dark skin sista with the nice curves, Shane?" Belle asked, incredulously.

"The one and only," Falcon replied. "I think we've decided to give this a try and one thing led to another and I couldn't control it."

"Hoo boy." Topaz muttered. "You need a leash for your freak, man. Shane does not seem the type."

Falcon shrugged. "I guess we'll find out tonight, huh?"

Belle leaned in. "Cap'n, traverse this new journey with her careful—am talking eggshell careful. You know what I mean?"

Falcon nodded.

"She's your girl." Belle told him. "She's had your back. But if you break her heart she will cut you."

"Cut me?" Falcon couldn't help laughing. "I have no intentions of hurting her. Right now we seem to want the same things. If we aren't sexually compatible then we will have to talk about things and see what we can salvage but right now—I tell you I want this woman. I look at her and think back to Shannon and the differences…"

"Scary, huh?" Topaz chuckled.

"You have no idea. When Shannon and I kissed I rarely felt anything. There were no crazy, romance novel spark. I kissed Shane once and my whole body was set on fire. Corny, I know but it's how I felt and how I feel thinking about it."

"Aww!" Belle cheered. "Well, maybe start out soft—because you don't know what she's like as a lover and the same for her."

Falcon nodded in agreement.

CHAPTER SEVEN

All day long, Shane wondered if she should give in or give up. Then again, all her dating life she'd tried finding a good man. All those men blew up in her face—not in a good way. They were either too sleazy or too creepy, one was married with five girls. Apparently he thought cheating on his wife would give him the boy he so desperately needed. She rolled her eyes at that memory while shaving her legs. To make that disaster even worse, the jerk wasn't even good in bed.

Shane sighed dramatically and rinsed her razor before setting in the holder before washing her body carefully. Then next forty five minutes was spent inspecting every inch of her body for any unwanted hair. If she was going to sleep with Falcon, it had to be perfect—she had to be perfect.

With her shower out of the way, Shane lathered on some unscented lotion, squirted some perfume against her neck and shoulders then sat down to slide her feet into a pair of silver Sergio Rossi Tresor heels. When she stood, her eyes caught her body in the mirror. Her breasts weren't as perky as a few years before and self consciousness kicked in. Maybe she should wear a bra—he'd understand. She tapped the sides of her boobs gently watching the way they jiggled.

But the heat in the way he'd ordered her to wear nothing else had her reaching for the coat and sliding her arms into it. Shane paid close attention to tying the straps carefully. The last thing she needed was for the damn thing to catch a good breeze and go flying open as she walked to her car.

The drive through the city was nerve-wracking at best. Each time someone from another vehicle glanced at her, Shane's heart raced painfully. She kept wondering if the coat had come undone and they could see her most private parts. A few times she even glanced down, just to make sure. An old lady pulled up beside her at a stoplight and their eyes met. Shane wondered if this woman knew what Shane was about to do? Hell, Shane didn't even know what she was about to do. But from the way Falcon wanted her dressed, Shane could probably guess it wasn't to have tea and cookies.

A part of her knew the woman knew. She eyed Shane with a look that spoke volumes. The strange thing about it was, though their connection only lasted perhaps a grand total of thirty seconds, Shane didn't care what this strange woman or anyone thought. Whether Falcon was testing her or had every intention of doing her bent over the kitchen table, Shane would take it.

She was ready for it.

She craved it.

You can't guilt me old lady! A happy voice inside her head shouted.

Shane offered the woman a smile, and a quick wave then turned back in time to see the light had changed. Glancing both ways to ensure traffic on either side had stopped, Shane drove her Wraith through the intersection.

Two minutes to eight, Shane pulled into Falcon's front yard. He was sitting on the top step, legs apart and elbows pressed against his knees. She killed the engine, withdrew the keys and dumped them into her purse. When she looked up again, he crooked a finger at her and motioned for her to come. After gathering her purse, she pushed from the leather seat and slammed the door. She'd barely taken two steps before he held up a hand. Instinctively, Shane stopped.

"Set your purse down on this step," Falcon instructed her.

He didn't move, but merely watched her with a heated stare that was both stern yet alluring. She began dripping down her legs and that startled her. Confused as to how her body could already be so wet, she did as he demanded and waited.

"You had questions about my sexual life. You are the one who always said *action speaks louder than words*. I'll show you. Then, you can decide if you wish to proceed or if we stop."

"Okay." Shane couldn't believe her tiny her voice sounded, how weak and quivering it was to her own ears. She cleared her throat.

"Undo the belt."

"Here?"

"Do not ask questions, Shane. Undo the belt."

Though her mind screamed at her to pick up her purse and leave, Shane's hands moved as if they had minds of their own, reaching up and tugging at the straps to her coat. When they were free, she met his eyes.

"Push it off your shoulders."

She barely hesitated. Soon the cool evening

air caressed her bare flesh. It felt so good to be free of it for the temperature had been smoldering. All the way there she felt as though she would erupt into flames with the thick coat against her skin. But that wasn't what made her moan. Knowing Falcon was staring at her, caressing her bare flesh with his eyes, that caused her to tremble and a groan to tumble from the deepest part of her core.

Shane finally looked at him. He watched her with something akin to a lion eyeing its prey.

Intently, obsessively.

Her nipples tighten. She tried covering them with her hands but he cleared his throat and straightened his spine.

"Why would you want to hide your body from me?"

"Why? Falcon, look at me." Shane frowned. "Be honest. Do I look like any of the women you've dated?"

"No."

"Okay then. Why do you want me to be

naked like this—on your front porch where anyone could walk by and see?"

"Because if we're to be lovers you have to know what turns me on."

"And the thought of getting caught..."

"Is a part of it. What I really wanted to see was the dying sun against your skin. I wanted to see if your whole body could be sun kissed."

"My body..."

"Shhh. Let me look at you."

Shane turned her head away and allowed him to continue until finally he approached her. She felt him moving closer and closer until she smelled the faint musk of his cologne. Falcon trailed a finger down between her breasts. That tender connection was everything and didn't last nearly as long. She whimpered when it was taken away. He moved around her, from time to time grazing her flesh with his finger or a nail. By the time he faced her again, Shane was a trembling, dripping mess.

"Do you want me to taste you, Shane?"

She gasped and lifted her gaze to meet his. There was no laughter in his eyes.

"Do you want my mouth and my tongue on your body?"

"Yes."

"Where?"

"Falcon, I can't..."

Before she knew what was happening, Falcon had her bent over the front railing. She felt exposed to his eyes with her ass hiked in the air and breasts pointing to the ground. There was no time to voice her concern for his large hand came down hard against one cheek then the next repeatedly. The first smack left her speechless with shock, the second had a kind of tingling sensation. The third time his work roughened hands landed against her flesh, Shane was so close to climaxing she had to bite her lower lip.

Falcon righted her and looked into her eyes. Her cheeks pulsed with the abuse he'd just bestowed on her and she had to admit she love over tingle of it.

"Can't—." He admonished. "That word doesn't exist in my bed. Let's try this again. Tell me where you want my mouth and my tongue."

Though tempted to disobey again just so he'd spank her once more, Shane licked her lips, folded her arms behind her back and sighed dreamily. "My nipples, my sides, between my legs…"

Falcon smiled at her and stepped in close. He licked his lips like a beast ready to devour his catch. But Falcon didn't ravish her like she'd hoped. No, instead he took his time. He started at the soft spot beneath her ear, licking, circling the flesh with his tongue and biting his way down between her breasts. Every inch he covered sent her heart beating faster in anticipation of what was to come.

When his mouth finally engulfed her left nipple, Shane could only give in to the pleasure it caused. Falcon wrapped his arm around her back as his hot, wet mouth picked up suction. Weak and helpless against his carnal assault, Shane gave in to everything he offered and handed over all he demanded. Her nipple hardened even further against his tongue as the stream against her legs quickened.

"Please…" Shane pleaded. "Falcon please…"

"Please?" He released her long enough to ask. "Tell me what you're pleading for, my sweet."

"Touch me."

Falcon found her wetness with a large finger and stroked, pinched and pulled against her tender jewel. It was even better with him doing that to her in person. In her head it had been good but nothing compared to having Falcon's hand, his fingers finding her most intimate folds and exploring. Shards of fire trailed her flesh, burrowed beneath her skin and charged her heart. Her breath escaped her body in loud gasps followed by exhilarated squeals.

Everything in that moment worked in concert to spur Shane on to a blissful finale. The air around her, cool against her heated flesh,

Falcon's smell, the manliness in which he took charge, even the hardness of his body. She opened herself and her legs up to Falcon, taking his finger deep and riding it as if her life depended on it. She chewed her lower lip, grind her teeth, all to keep the rising lava she knew was edging her control.

"You want to scream," Falcon whispered against her ear before biting her lobe. "It's okay to scream for me—in fact, I insist."

"The neighbours." Shane panted.

"Doesn't matter." Falcon told her, adding a second finger and hitting her spot each time he shoved them in.

Shane curled into him, shoving her face into his neck. "Damn baby!" She cried against his flesh even as her hips worked away to keep him as deeply as she needed him.

"You *will* scream for me," Falcon said, his voice husky.

Sinking her nails into his back through his shirt, Shane arched backward, fighting the crashing end she felt coming. But no matter how desperately she tried to behave, to be a good girl and remained quiet. No matter how much she fought letting him see just how much what he'd been doing to her aroused her. No matter how dearly she wanted to keep the fact that getting caught made her wet, it was all in vain. For when his mouth found her tender nipples again, all Shane could do was grip into Falcon for dear life, squeezed her eyes shut and give him what he demanded.

"Falcon!" She screamed, her voice carrying out away from them then echoing off her brain. Her legs gave out under her, her breasts throbbed sweetly along with the wet patched in her core. He slid the fingers into her again one final time before catching her and scooping her into his arms against his chest.

"Falcon..." Shane whispered, weak and trembling.

"Don't worry," he replied. "I got you."

It'd been hours since Shane had fallen asleep. Falcon retrieved her bag and coat from where they were on the front porch and set them on the sofa. For a while after he laid her on his bed, he watched. Shane's breathing was soft, her nostrils flared whenever she exhaled and the corners of her lips would twitch ever so often.

So many times before he'd been around her as she snoozed, even be in the same bed with her. But he knew after the line they'd crossed earlier, there was no going back to that long ago comfort.

He stood at the window watching the sky light up with lightening and hearing the harsh roll of thunder. He toyed with a pair of handcuffs he purchased a while back because he wanted a back-up pair for work but never used them. As a matter of fact, after the crap he went through trying to open the damn thing, he'd just chucked them on the dresser in his room. When they were delivered, Falcon spent the better part of five minutes muttering every profanity under his breath as he fought with the plastic case they came in. Eventually, he'd gone down to the kitchen, grabbed a pair of scissors and cut through the top.

The cuffs glistened in the rainy glow of the moon, tempting him to give in the primal thoughts going through his mind of all the wonderfully carnal things he could do with the restrains.

Touch me.

Shane's pleasure soften voice had demanded. That was a part of her he never got to see and suddenly he was jealous of the men who had. She was alive in his arms, demanding to be pleasured. He'd spanked her, felt his hand sink into the perfectly rounded, dark brown flesh of her ass. When he lifted his palm, his brand remained on her flesh and he wished everyone could see it and knew she was his. He'd lost control when he realize it made her so wet, she had been draining down her legs to puddle on the ground. It was easy to be consumed by that sensation. The thought of knowing he could make her melt for him. Her scent was strong and though he wanted desperately to taste her, to feel her sitting atop his face until her climax caused her to slide off his face, Falcon knew he had to stay in control as best he could. He had to hold it together and seduce her slowly.

His marriage to Shannon hadn't worked and Falcon knew one of the main reasons was because Shannon wasn't particularly sexual. Before they said I Do, Shannon could go anywhere any time. Sure, she wasn't adventurous in bed but after Danielle was born, Shannon's legs closed so fast and hard, he still had whiplash. Falcon figured he could understand—giving birth must have scared her but they could have talked about it. They could have used protection.

After a while, he stopped expecting anything. Falcon couldn't make that same mistake, not with Shane. He'd gone so long without being intimate with anyone that the thought of being with Shane scared him. But the moment she dropped that coat and it puddle on the ground, Falcon was sure he couldn't walk away if he tried.

No, this time had to be different. With Shane he had to be slow and calculated because seducing Shane was as much to ensure her and Falcon were sexually compatible as much as anything else.

Thunder rolled across the sky and Falcon turned to look at the bed where Shane was tangled in the sheets. The room lit up from lightening and she rolled over causing the sheets to slip down. One breast came free and Falcon licked his lips while fingering the hard metal of the cuffs. Shane had soft breasts. They were perfectly, chocolaty brown with Hershey kiss nipples that tightened against his tongue wonderfully.

He approached the bed and leaning in to caress her left arm as he lifted it above her head. Gently, he cuffed her to the metal headboard before doing the same with her other hand. He slid the sheets from the bed leaving her bare and beautiful beneath his eyes. Falcon removed his shirt then knelt between her legs on the bed, caressing her flesh gently. He trailed his fingers up her legs to the inside of her thighs and when she squired, he retreated.

Once he had been sure she was sleeping again, he leaned in and kissed her, gaining entrance to her mouth by teasing her lips with his tongue until she sighed. Unable to control himself, Falcon felt his eyes rolled into his head as she awoke and returned his kiss. Then she started tugging on the cuffs and he pushed himself up and looked down to see panic in her beautiful, brown gaze.

"Do you want to get free?" Falcon asked, stroking the underside of her breasts with a tender finger tip.

"What is this?" She asked.

"Say the word, Shane and I'll undo them. But you might want to see what I have in mind for you first."

She stopped struggling.

Without another word, Falcon slipped down her body, dragging his tongue as he went. He stopped to nibble her nipples, to kiss the valley between those perfect mounds then continued on his mission. The destination was her heated center. He spread her legs wider, licked his lips and kissed the insides of her thighs. Falcon swirled his tongue in circles against the flesh, tasting remnants of what he'd made her do earlier. It was just as he thought—Shane was delicious.

Growling, he licked at her intimately.

She gasped.

He sucked on her, sliding his tongue in and out, lapping at her, daring her to resist him. Instead, Shane exhaled loudly, and Falcon gave himself over to the beauty before him. The sound of her tugging at the cuffs, trying to get loose as he slurped at her, was like music to his ears. He loved the metal on metal, the soft gasps from her mouth, the quiver in the way she said his name.

She did melt on his tongue, tangy and hot. It was as if he couldn't get enough.

"Falcon!" She gasped. "Lick me! More, please!"

Her cries pushed him, drove him to do more. Though his arousal pressed painfully into his pants, Falcon was too far gone catering to her needs, answering the movement of her body and pushing her closer to the edge. He reached up to fondle her breasts, even as he plunged his tongue deep into her.

"Yes! Baby…"

Her whole body went stiff then, as the room lit up with lightning and thunder rattled around and above them, Shane screamed while her body shuddered. Her legs shook so hard, Falcon had to hold them against the bed. Then, without warning, Shane dripped down his chin. He kept his mouth on her until she went limp on the bed. Falcon released her and sat back to watch her body heave from what he'd done to her. She was so beautiful in that moment Falcon couldn't help the surge of pride that filled him.

He removed the cuff from her and pulled her into his arms.

Chapter Eight

The sun shining into Shane's face woke her up. She moaned wondering if her sister had moved her room around again. The last time Francine had just taken a trip to China and some jerk taught her feng shui. Shane moaned and rolled over to hide from the annoyance when her body crashed into someone.

Shane smiled. She remembered what happened the night before—of being spanked until she almost came. Then to add to her pleasure, he'd cuffed her, took away her control then feasted on her as if she was his last supper. The memory made her tremble and pulled an involuntary groan from her body. She cuddled closer to him, resting her head against his chest and listening to his heart humming beneath her ear. His skin was warm against her face, soothing her. Just because she could, Shane tossed a possessive arm across him then dragged her palm up his side, over the scar he'd gotten trying to break up a bar fight. One of the assailants had a knife. That day she was terrified at first. Then when she found out he was going to be okay she lashed out, calling him a moron for pulling a stunt like that. In the end he deflated her with one very short sentence—I'm a cop.

He shifted under her, wrapping an arm around her and Shane smiled. For the first time in her dating life, it was as if she was supposed to be right there, in Falcon's arms. The urge to quickly grab her things and scramble out the front door was nowhere in her. She studied him for a while, trying to find a reason to regret their night together. She'd allowed this man to boss her around, to bend her over a railing and spanked her and she wasn't even sorry. Hell, she got wet again just thinking of his hand raining down against her cheeks.

Shane squirmed.

Pushing to her elbow, she looked down into his face. A few years before, she would have had to push hair out of the way to see his eyes. Falcon cut his hair so his helmet would fit better. The truth was, no matter if he had long hair or not, Falcon was so good looking she was helpless at the thought of it.

Unable to help herself, Shane leaned forward and kissed at his neck, traced her lips along his collarbone then up to his chin.

"Shane…"

Shane lifted her head but he wasn't awake. Knowing he knew her touch did something amazing to her. Grinning, she climbed from the bed and hurried into the bathroom. Though she had no toothbrush or anything at Falcon's place, she improvised by pushing toothpaste onto her finger and rubbed her teeth with it. After rinsing her mouth, she gargled some mouth wash—twice—then rinsed her mouth. Testing her breath the old fashion way, by blowing into her palm and sniffing it, Shane was satisfied her breath wouldn't stop a Mack Truck. Humming to herself, she climbed into the bathtub. She sang to herself, the first time she'd done that in a while. Happiness felt good.

After a quick shower, she carefully dried her skin then went through his cabinet for a bottle of lotion she'd left there a while back. She couldn't find it so she wrapped a towel around her hips and tiptoed down the hall to Danielle's room. Thankfully she was spending the night at her best friend, Charlie's, so Shane took some lotion and lathered her skin. Thankfully it was scentless so all she had to do was rummage through her purse for a bottle of cologne and squirted some on her neck. When she hurried back into the bedroom, Falcon had rolled over to his stomach.

Shane figured she had a couple of hours before he had to really be up and about so she had to hurry. Dropping the towel, she climbed on the bed and sat astride him, pressing intimately against his ass. Leisurely, she traced her fingers down his back, over the tattoos while slowly writhing her hips against him.

"Falcon." She whispered. "Wake up."

When he only moaned and went back to sleep, she rooted her hips lower, digging deeper. "Falcon."

"It's too early baby," Falcon whispered. "Go back to sleep."

"Seriously?" Shane asked, leaning forward and kissing his ear. "Early? I'm naked, sitting on your back. There are so many more wonderful things we could be doing right now. But, sure, I could let you go back to bed."

"Tease."

"You don't think I'm naked?" She shimmied, making sure her nipples caress his back all the while grinding her hips against his ass.

"Damn, Shane. You're already wet."

She giggled but rolled off his back to lie down beside him. He instantly reached over and dragged a fingertip against her intimately. As she moaned, he pushed the finger past her lips and into the hot wetness of her body. "You called me baby." She whispered.

Falcon shuffled on the bed to kneel beside her. "I did." He worked the finger in and out of her slowly.

"Oh Falcon, deeper."

"What about me calling you baby?"

"I like it." She was breathy. Shane reached up and caught him behind the neck. She brought his head down so his mouth hovered above her breast. "Suck it." She demanded softly. "Please."

"You started this seduction, Shane." Falcon licked at the tightening bud. "No need to be polite. You want your pleasure—take it."

"And you're sure about this?" Shane sighed.

"Very."

She eased away from him and climbed out of the bed. When Shane glanced over her shoulder, he'd pushed to his elbows and was watching her with dark, unreadable eyes. With a wink, Shane moved to his closet and pulled out one of his ties. Without a word, she returned to the bed, and lifted it. "Close your eyes."

Falcon did as she told him and in a gentle motion, she pulled the tie over his head and blindfolded him. Satisfied he couldn't see, Shane pushed him to his back on the bed then climbed astride him. All she really wanted was to feel him inside her, to have him hot and trembling around her. But as Shane watched him lying there, eyes covered, muscles shivering to each drag of her fingertips, she gave her heart and head a break and allowed her body to take over.

It started with the swirl of her tongue against his pecs then slowly down further. She nibbled against him while listening to his breathing quicken. Falcon tried reaching for her but Shane merely took his hands and pressed them into the bed on both his sides.

"Shane…" He called.

She could hear the frustration in his voice, felt his passion for her in that one utterance. But Shane wasn't ready to give up her exploration of his body. Each time she released his arms, he tried touching again, to wrap his arms around her. Whenever that happens she only pushed them away, then went back to tasting him, flicking her tongue against each patch of flesh she could reach. But soon, teasing him became too much for her and no matter how much she tried ignoring the fire raging inside her, there was no putting it off.

Finally, she grabbed a condom from his bedside table and ripped the packet open with her teeth. As she rolled it on to him, she watched his face. His tongue passed over his lips and then they parted as if in anticipation of what he knew was coming. Shane was helpless as she grabbed him and guided him to her entrance. With her eyes closed, she pressed down, gasping as he filled her completely. Shane gripped her hips then and though she wanted to move his hands away, Shane was too far gone to care. She gave him control to roll her hips as he needed, to go fast, then slow, then fast again. Each tip of her pelvic had him crashing into her spot, repeatedly until she was dizzy and digging her nails into his chest.

"Falcon I want..." The few words escaped her lips but Shane couldn't seem to wrap her mind around what she wanted. Each time she tried speaking her voice came out in an audible moan. She gave up and allowed the climax that pulsed from the tips of her toes all the way through her core to ravage her body. Each inhalation was like sweet fire and every time she exhaled it was as if she would die from it. His large fingers were pressed into her flesh and he held her down against him as she squeezed him tightly.

Falcon grunted something but Shane was in such a wonderful place, as if she was high on what he did to her, she couldn't decipher what it was. When she began floating back to earth, Falcon made his move.

"What do you want?" Falcon asked, grabbing her waist and flipping her to her back on the bed.

"I..." Shane was still weak.

He caressed up her body and found her nipples and tugged. Shane cried out for him and his name trailed off into a whimper.

"Tell me what you want!"

"More..."

Without removing the blindfold, Falcon flipped her to her stomach. "On your knees," he demanded. His voice sounded hard and straining with control. Shane got caught up in it so she hesitated. His large palm fell hard against her ass. Shane mewled in pleasure but snapped to and pushed to her knees.

"Good girl," he said. "Spread your legs."

He found her entrance with a finger then with his arousal and entered her again. This time when his large palm made its way up Shane's back, it was to grab a fistful of her hair. He used the hold on her to pull her back into him. Shane closed her eyes, tilt her head back and enjoy him slamming into her repeatedly. She tried crying out, to plead with him for more, harder, deeper anything but he'd taken her breath away. It was the best feeling like sitting in a rollercoaster going a million miles a minute then dropping. And though she tried screaming, she couldn't because the adrenaline was so good, all she could do was bite into her lower lip. In no time at all, Shane's world shattered and he released her hair but his hips didn't slow.

She couldn't breathe and she didn't care. Her hair was a mess but she didn't give a damn. All she cared about was the sensations stampeding through her veins, leaving her a whimpering mess in Falcon's bed.

This time, however, Falcon grunted and pulled away from her. She quickly turned around to see him kneeling at the foot of the bed and pulling the condom off. His eyes were trained on her as he wrapped a fight fist around himself.

"Need a little help, darling?" Shane asked.

He smirked at her. "Sit back, spread your legs and look at me. Can you do that?"

Shane swallowed and blinked. Did he really want her to watch while he…She'd never done that before and though the thought of it made her hot, Shane wondered what good could possible come of it. But she remembered what happened the last time she disobeyed in Falcon's bed. He spanked her until she climaxed. Shane was tempted to say no but the way his pecs twitched, the way his body tightened, she knew he needed release. So instead, she did as he asked, she pressed her back to the headboards and spread her legs for him.

As she watched him, Falcon's eyes caressed up her body, from one leg to the next. He looked at her more intimately than anyone else, his eyes leaving her body heated and ready to break again. While he stared, he touched himself, caressing his abs, up over his nipples to his neck then down again. He stroke himself in long, slow pulls at first. Shane licked her lips, desperate to reach across the small space and touch him, taste him, anything.

"Falcon..."

He arched his head back, grunted her name and his world seem to fall apart. Hot, white released flew across the space, some landing on the top of her left leg, some against her stomach and the rest on the bed. No matter how nervous Shane was about this scenario, she couldn't deny how hot it was or how beautiful Falcon looked as his massive body tensed then shook powerfully. Finally, after sitting back for as long as she could, Shane eased across to him, wrapped her arms around his frame and snuggled her head beneath his chin.

"We can't go back, Shane," he said, shivering into her body. "We can't... we have to do this again. I can't resist you."

She laughed softly. "I don't want to go back, Falcon." Shane kissed his shoulder. "I'll follow your lead."

SURRENDER—Prey

CHAPTER NINE

The week slipped by with Falcon and his team helping the local police carry out a series of raids on illegal pot dens all over the city. Though he saw his daughter, he hadn't had time to spend with Shane. They talked on the phone but each time they made plans, they fell through because work got in the way. After a while, he could sense a strained between them and he knew why. He knew Shane like he knew the back of his hands and he could imagine what was going through her head. Falcon knew she probably thought he was backing out.

He slammed the locker shut and flopped to the bench to push his feet into a pair of socks then his sneakers. At that point he had to wonder if Shane was ready for the type of job he did.

Sure, it was fine when he wasn't dating her. She would step in and look in on Danielle for him while he was away on a collar. Shane would always be there for whatever he or Danielle needed. Surely she understood that they could be in the middle of making love and the phone rings and he'd have to go. But, he saw where she was coming from. The beginning of every relationship is important and for him to always be gone, that wasn't much of a beginning.

"You okay, boss?" Belle asked.

Falcon looked up at her and smiled sadly. She was really quite beautiful—dark skin, big brown eyes, and a round face that was framed with short black hair. She rarely left her hair down. He smiled tightly. "I'm not sure."

She sat beside him. "Okay. What's up?"

"Um—Shane and I are seeing each other."

"Well shit, finally!" Belle cheered. "So why the long face?"

"We've been keeping it a secret—trying to find our footing. But over the past week work just kept getting the way. Now I feel her pulling away from me."

"Yeah. Hence the reason I've been single." Belle took a breath. "This job, Falcon—this job takes more than it gives and sometimes, when I'm alone at nights I wonder if this is all there is to life. I wonder if it's worth it to keep doing this only to be alone at nights."

"But I love this job."

"Well, now you need to decide if you love it more than you care for her. Falcon, listen, if you want this woman you can make it work with her and the job. You're just going to have to put in a little more effort that the guy out there who has the typical nine to face. You're going to have to prove to her that even though what you do is important to you, seeing her smile is just as big in your world."

"She knows that."

"Does she?"

Falcon sighed. He had been out of the dating game for too long. "What are you saying?"

"I'm saying, you thinking she knows and you actually telling her are two different things. Romance her. Show her that she matters. And keeping your being together a secret isn't helping. I'm sure your daughter won't mind."

"How are you so sure?"

"Well, Danielle is a smart kid. Give her a chance to show you."

"Yeah." A plan began forming inside Falcon's head. "I guess you're right."

"Of course, I'm right. I'm a woman." Belle laughed and patted his thigh. "Now, get up and go home. Spend some time with your baby then head on over to Shane's and—you know? Talk?"

Falcon nodded with a smile. "Thanks Belle. And could you keep the info about Shane's and my relationship…"

"What relationship?"

Falcon laughed and bumped fists with her. She left him to head to her locker and he grabbed his bag, tossed it over his shoulder and exited the change room. But he didn't go straight home. He stopped at a flower shop and put in an order then headed home. The house was empty—no Shane, no Danielle, nothing but coldness. He took a shower, checked his voicemail then sat in the kitchen, back against the island, drinking a beer. He wondered what he'd done in a previous life to deserve any of this—the pain he heard in Shane's voice broke his heart.

Perhaps he'd been imagining it. Maybe he was just feeling guilty for not spending as much time with her as he knew he should have. Either way, something had to give. He cared for Shane. When he was in her arms, in her bed he felt alive and he hadn't had that ever. Not even with Shannon, Danielle's mother. Sure, Falcon thought he loved her but it hadn't been love. She didn't curl his toes just by watching him touch himself. Shannon would never have gone for that and after a few years their sex life just disappeared.

Falcon nodded, needlessly. With Shane, he had to do better. He had to love her like a man was supposed to love a woman—purely.

Her night with Danielle was different. She knew Falcon wanted to wait until their relationship was steady before bringing Danielle into it but Shane couldn't help imagining. Sure, Danielle liked her as God-mother but would the teenager want her as a mother? Shane shook her head. It didn't matter what she wanted or how excited she was, Danielle was Falcon's child and he knew what was best for his baby. Besides, that decision was probably for the best since her and Falcon hadn't really gotten together in about a week and a half.

His work was always calling, cutting into their plans and Shane expected that. She'd never been jealous of his job, ever and she knew that would be one of the side effects of dating a cop. But she couldn't shake the feeling he wanted out. Taking a deep breath, Shane placed the large sketchpad she'd purchased for Danielle before her on the island.

"You got me a present?" Danielle asked.

"It's a little something," Shane replied. "I know you said your other one was almost full and an artist cannot run out of space, you know."

Danielle hugged her. "Thank you."

"Listen, I was talking to Anisa and she suggested something. Her suggestion was that I ask you to design a wedding gown for me. If I like it, we have it manufactured by one of our contacts and we sell it exclusively in my store...."

Danielle began flailing.

"We figured you could use it on your application for the Fashion Institute. Now, the deal is this—seventy percent of the money we make from your dress will be added to your trust fund. Ten percent would be for you to do with as you see fit and twenty will be going toward that car I know you want. What do you think?"

"Did you run it by dad?"

Shane nodded.

"Then I'm in!" Danielle beamed then

snatched up her new sketchpad. "I'll start right now!"

Before Shane could say anything, her God daughter took off up the stairs yelling something about if Shane didn't see her down in two hours to send a search party. Shane laughed. "Okay, I know the perfect cops for the job too!"

Danielle giggled.

Shane shook her head and went back to her coffee and to leafing through a catalogue. She'd used the company before to pick a few gowns that went like hot cakes. Hopefully she could go for a repeat. It took her a couple of hours to get through all the catalogues that were sitting on her desk. Once she sent out emails for the orders, she hurried into the kitchen, poured two glasses of milk and grabbed a box of unopened Oreos. She found Danielle in the guestroom a bunch of paper crunched up and in a pile at the foot of the bed. She had her tongue stuck out the side of her mouth as she scribbled away. Shane grinned—Falcon did the same thing when he concentrated too hard.

"I brought snacks," Shane said.

Danielle quickly closed the pad. "You can't see it yet."

"Oh…kay. Sure." She entered and set the milk on the bedside table before climbing to sit on the bed with Danielle. "What time does your father want you home?"

"I'm not sure but I probably should get going soon." Danielle accepted the milk. "I have French homework and I left it. I finished the Math and Social Studies but forgot the French."

"Okay. Let's finish eating these then we can stop by Olanti's and pick up some dinner on our way home. Maybe Falcon will be there and we can have something to eat."

"Their Lemon Chicken is to die for."

"I take it you know what you want?"

"Yup!" Danielle crunched into a cookie. "I really hope this gown comes out nicely. This is a huge opportunity."

"Girl, don't put too much stress on yourself

about it. We can always tweak and make things work. This is supposed to be fun."

"I know. But it's also a chance to show dad I can do this."

"I'm not a hundred percent sure, maybe about ninety nine point nine nine percent sure your father thinks you're Wonder Woman."

Danielle laughed.

"What I'm trying to say is your father has confidence in you. I have confidence in you and so does Francine—hell even Charlie. You're the only one who doesn't see how fantastic and talented you are."

"I don't want to be egotistic."

"Trust me, sweetie." Shane touched her cheek gently. "Sometimes, my dear, a little ego is a marvelous thing. It reminds us that we are wonderful creatures and we need to own up to that."

Danielle grinned, set her milk aside and hugged Shane. Shane held onto Danielle, knowing this hug was better than all the other ones she'd received from the teenager. She held the back of Danielle's head, fighting the burning of unshed tears in her eyes. When she released Danielle, they retrieved their glasses and delved into the cookies. They were talking about everything under the sun when the doorbell echoed through the house. Shane excused herself and hurried down to open the door to a delivery man.

"Delivery for Shane Teller," he said.

"Um—I'm Shane Teller."

"Wonderful, sign here, please."

Shane accepted the clipboard and signed then handed it back. When he gave her the beautiful bouquet, Shane closed the door and wandered into the kitchen. She had no idea who they were from. Setting the glass vase on the counter, she rummaged around through the get up and found a card.

Shane, I know I haven't been around like I used to. But it's not because I don't want to be. I can do better. I promise.

Birdman

Tears filled her eyes and it took her a moment to pull it together. But, Shane shoved the card into her back pocket, sniffed at the roses and hummed to herself as she jogged up the stairs back to Danielle.

"Who was that?" Danielle asked.

"Delivery."

It was about an hour later when they finally showered and got it together to head back to Falcon's. They detoured by Danielle's favorite take out joint for some dinner for all three, as well as a nearby bakery for a carrot cake. When they made it home, Falcon was shirtless, had the hood of the truck open and bent over it with an oily rag sticking out of his oil covered jeans.

For a moment she sat in the car, staring at him. She remembered the way that perfect body felt against her, wrapped around her, diving into her. Gripping the door handle was all she could do to avoid moaning. Though she tried not ogling the man, Shane was pretty sure she failed—especially when he caught her looking and smirked. Falcon pulled the rag from his pocket and walked toward her car. Danielle climbed out and she did the same, praying her knees wouldn't give out.

"No hug for your old man?" Falcon asked Danielle.

"Dad, this dress is Givenchy," Danielle said. "I can't have you get oil all over it. But I can offer a kiss."

Falcon beamed like a fool when Danielle dropped a chaste kiss to his lips.

"We brought food," Danielle added. "Let me take it inside."

"Thanks, Danielle," Shane said.

Voice didn't crack! Score!

"Hi," Falcon said, reaching in to kiss her.

Shane instinctively took a step backward.

"What's the matter?" Falcon asked. "I wasn't going to get oil on you or anything. It's just a kiss."

"Um—I wasn't sure if Danielle was inside

yet." Shane's cheeks flushed. "Sorry."

"Don't be," Falcon whispered, leaning in again.

This time Shane gave him her mouth. She enjoyed the thickness of his lips, the smell of his body, the caress of his breath against her skin. Her knees wobbled and she clutched at his shoulders. Falcon pressed a large palm to the center of her back and in that moment, in her daze and heated want of him, she'd completely forgotten his hands were covered in sludge from fixing his truck.

In all honesty, Shane didn't care. She merely flung herself into the kiss until she couldn't breathe. "Thank you for the flowers," Shane said. "But you know Danielle could have seen them."

"I know. I don't want to hide us anymore." Falcon nibbled at her shoulder. "It's not like you're some strange. You've known her since she was a baby."

"I suppose—but can we not tell her tonight?" Shane said. "Let's eat some food and then I can have one more night to think about this."

"Think about it?" Falcon arched a brow. "I don't understand. I thought you wanted an us."

"I do. But you can't begrudge a girl some nerves. After you tell her there is no going back and she could hate me."

"Shane I don't think…"

"But you never know." She looped her arm with his. "Let's go inside."

Falcon said nothing. Once they were inside, the three worked together to set out dinner. Falcon got wine ready while Shane opened a box of apple juice so Danielle could have some. They sat at the dinner table and ate like a family. It was a moment Shane wanted to hold on to and never let go. But over the next little while, anything could happen.

"Dad, aunt Francine texted me this morning," Danielle said. "She wants to know if I could come over to her place and spend some time with her. I know it's a school night tomorrow but she promises to drop me off at school in the squad car."

Shane choked and Falcon peered at her. She had no idea Francine did that. Shane knew what her sister was doing. Francine was trying to get them some time alone together. She smile and cleared her throat.

"I don't see why not. Did you finish your homework?" Falcon asked.

"Not yet. But I'll be finished by the time her shift is over later today. I already did the reading. I just have to answer some questions."

"Okay," Falcon said.

"Can I be excused?" Danielle asked. "I'll have desert later."

"Sure," Falcon replied.

Danielle eased from the table, stopped to hug Shane then darted off up the stairs. Shane licked her lips and stared at Falcon who was chewing slowly.

"You know what she's doing right?" Shane asked.

"Yeah. Your sister is trying to play Cupid."

"I've been talking to her about how I've been feeling." Shane sipped her wine. "I know your work is important to you and I understand why you do it. I know what it's like having you get up in the middle of the night and leave. I know what it's like to have plans with you and duty calls. I don't know why I was so upset…"

"Baby, you're upset because we're new. Can I make you a deal?"

Shane arched a brow. "Okay."

"At least once a week, we'll take some time and be together," Falcon said. "And when we're with each other, that is our time."

"You can't make that promise. And I don't expect you to."

"What're we doing tonight?"

"I was going to head over to the Belegin Hotel and have a spa night. I have a room booked."

"Do you mind if I stopped by?"

Shane grinned. "Not at all. Since you're

coming I have to make some preparations."

"Oh really? Can I be privy to these?"

She grinned and picked up her plate and his. Though she wanted to tell him, Shane figured she'd keep it a surprise. In the kitchen, Falcon caught her and trapped her against the island. He took the plates from her and set them to the side before bracing his palms into the counter. She sighed and tilted her neck to the side, giving him access to nibble away.

"I don't want to wait until tonight," Falcon confessed. "I want you now."

"I can feel that." Shane moaned. "But Danielle is upstairs…"

"I know." Falcon buried his face into her neck. "I'm going to confess something to you. I've never wanted another woman the way I want you. Does it make me a horrible person that I didn't want me wife like this?"

"What kind of person does it makes me that I love hearing that?"

Falcon kissed her again. She sensed the

conflict he was experiencing in that moment, the guilt of not wanting Shannon desperately. But whereas Falcon could have worked things out with Shannon, she took off and left him to raise their daughter on his own. "I'm sorry. I probably shouldn't have said that."

"We can't carry this guilt into our relationship with us."

"I agree."

Falcon sighed, kissed her one final time and released her. They finished putting the plates in the dishwasher and she sipped on a glass of water as he added the cleaner and started it. Once that was going, she turned her back to him and pressed her eyes closed.

"I'm going to head out," Shane said, taking a final drink from her glass and setting it on the counter.

"Shane…"

"Remember me saying I had some preparation to put together?" Shane turned and leveled her gaze on him. "I'm not running. Meet me at the hotel for eight-ish?"

Falcon smiled. "Okay. Eight-ish."

"I'm serious, Falcon."

He nodded. "I know."

Shane kissed him once, twice and then a third time. Though she knew she had to go, Shane clung to Falcon, kissing him repeatedly.

"Baby." Falcon laughed softly. "I know you don't want to go but…"

"I know." She kissed him again. "I know."

Shane released him and went to grab her purse. Though she should just leave, she rushed back, met him at the door leading to the kitchen and kissed him again. Finally, she hurried out the door without looking back. If she did, Shane knew there would be no leaving and Danielle would definitely find out about them. After she climbed behind the wheel, she slipped on her seatbelt, started the car and sped from the driveway. As she made her way toward her house she called her sister.

"I know what you're doing," Shane said

when Francine answered.

"Oh?" Francine said. "I don't know what you're talking about."

"You taking Danielle tonight? You knew I was going to have a spa night at the hotel and you think it would be a good idea for Falcon to be free so he could come."

Francine laughed. "Come on, Sis. I know how you feel about this guy. And I know you two haven't had much time to spend together lately. This is an important stage in your relationship—even though I haven't had a man in years even I know that."

"Franny?"

"Yeah?"

"You okay?"

Francine sighed. "Yeah. We can talk about it later. Right now, you shouldn't be talking to me. You should be getting things ready. I made an appointment at *Ex-Inhibitions* for you."

"Oh boy."

"A girl can never go wrong with lingerie.

That's all I'm saying."

Shane laughed. "Thanks, Franny. I love you!"

"Love you too. Now, once you get a breather from your stud, we should get together."

"It's a date."

Chapter Ten

Waiting for eight that night was torture. Falcon spent the time after Danielle hugged him and climbed into the front seat of Francine's car, pacing like a caged cat. Even though he wasn't sure what Shane had in mind, he hoped she wanted to give herself to him, to moan from his attention and open herself to him. He trembled at the memory of her falling apart under his fingers and his tongue.

Falcon loved the sounds she made, the way his name tumbled from her lips in gasps, soft whispers and screams that echoed all around them. But after so long, he couldn't believe how beautiful she was, how engaging, and loving she was as a lover. It surprised him—maybe because as a friend she'd been loyal and kind. He never expected her to be into what he was into—to want what he ached to do to her.

If Falcon was being honest, he'd admit showing her that side of him terrified him. The last thing he wanted was to lose her. But Shane was on fire in his arms.

He turned and looked at the clock. It was barely after seven and Falcon felt like screaming. To keep himself occupied, Falcon made his way into the office to paying some bills. He figured that would eat up a big chuck of time but he was wrong. When he finished paying all the bills and looked up, ten minutes had passed.

Eventually, it was seven thirty. Hurrying up the stairs, he grabbed a strip of condoms and dumped them into the side of his bag. He'd packed a few things for the night, including toiletries. After ensuring he had his credit card and some cash on him, Falcon hurried out the door.

The drive to the hotel was a relatively short one. Falcon used the time to pull himself together. Though a few times he wondered what she had in mind for him, he had to focus on the road. At the hotel, he gave the car to the valet, accepted his ticket and jogged up the steps. At the front desk he asked for her room and was directed to the elevator. The attendant carried him all the way to the sixtieth floor, then instructed him on where he needed to be. As he knocked on the dark, red door, Falcon felt his heart racing like never before. It was as though this was his first time meeting a woman at a hotel, the first time he'd give himself to her or the first time he'd be with any woman.

"Who is it?" Shane asked.

"It's Falcon…"

"Birdman, come in. It's open."

Falcon glanced around him before turning the knob and stepping into the room. The lights were low, but he could make out a path of rose petals leading from the door onward. Stopping for a second, Falcon set the *do not disturb* sign on the door and locked it. He dropped his bag to the floor, kicked off his shoes then followed the trail. "Baby?" He called.

He found her in the living room of the suite, and he almost passed out when he saw her. Falcon allowed his eyes to trail from the knee high gladiator heels she wore, up her legs, past her shapely thighs and over her beautiful curves, accentuated by a black corset. At the neck, her breasts pulsed at the top. Each time she inhaled they raised upward toward her chin then fell with her exhalation. Falcon couldn't believe how good she looked and when his arousal began straining against his pants, he had to chew against his bottom lip to keep control.

The rest of her was equally as sexy, the red of her lips, the curve of her lashes, the handcuffs hanging off her right index finger. He almost lost his breath then. Did she want him to use those on her?

"No," Shane told him. "These are for you."

Falcon tilted his head.

"Turnabout is fair play—isn't that what they

say?" Shane asked.

He couldn't speak. Knowing she was about to take his control turned him on even more. He kept his eyes fused to hers, trying to read her, to see what she was thinking. That didn't work. Instead, he licked his lips and waited.

"Sit on the floor, Falcon." Shane's voice dripped with honey. "With your back against the sofa."

He hesitated.

"Are you looking for a spanking?" Shane asked. "You know what happens when we disobey."

Falcon smirked.

"I hope you have no plans for the rest of the night."

"No." He crumbled to the floor to do as she ordered. "I'm all yours."

"Good."

She walked away from him to the far side of the room and still holding the cuffs, she turned her back to him, braced her palms to the wall and shook her hips. She swayed them from the right to the left, gyrating, rolling her body with the practiced ease of a dancer. Falcon's heart skipped a beat, his mouth went dry and his tongue stuck to the roof of his mouth. Shane backed up, glanced at him over her shoulder before bending forward, slowly, caressing her left leg all the way down.

Falcon moaned and tilted his head, trying to see what was beneath the black, lacey. boy cut panties she wore. But the movement gave nothing away and Falcon growled with frustration. She stood up once more and turned to face him, continuing her dance as their eyes locked. Falcon couldn't sit still anymore. He wanted to touch her, to hold her down against the floor and took what he needed from her body.

"Sit!" Shane demanded and Falcon slipped back to the floor.

She was closer now, the smell of *Opium* by Yves St. Larent floated through his nose to his brain. He'd never been so aroused by a woman's scent but it was playing havoc on his senses. Falcon reached forward again and to stop him, Shane lifted a heeled foot, pressed it against his chest and eased him back to his ass.

"Shane, you're killing me."

"Not yet." She smirked lowering her foot to the ground and stepping forward. She stood over him, a leg on each side of his own until each time she breathed her body brushed against his face. Falcon was so hard by this time, all he could do was sit there, helpless, weak and waiting.

Leaning around him, Shane restrained his arms with the cuffs then leisurely nibbled at his shoulder, his throat before dropping a kiss to each of his nipples. Falcon trembled, moaned, whimpered as he struggled to get free. Her flesh was soft against him and he knew he'd die if he couldn't touch her.

Shane slowly slipped down into her haunches and as her body passed his mouth, he stuck his tongue out, tasting her as she went. He licked a wet path down her body until they were face to face. Shane kissed him then, a searing smooth that had him panting and reaching up to tangle his fingers in her hair. He remembered the first time he did that. Shane hadn't been scared. She'd merely smirked at him and rode him harder. This time, she detangled his fingers from her hair and handcuffed his arms behind his back. Once that was done, Shane stood, turned around and bend over before his face.

Falcon ground his teeth, tugging at the restraints, wishing he could slide his hands up her smooth legs then test the wetness between them before pushing as hard and as deep into her as he could. Instead, he flicked his tongue out and she moaned. He sucked at her through the soft material of her panties, feasting on her and enjoying the way she tasted.

"Falcon." She sighed, bracing her hands against his legs, and wiggling herself against his tongue. Shane rolled her hips back and forth sliding her tender bud over his tongue. Each time it passed, Falcon sucked, and loved the moaned it elicited from her body. He could tell when she was close to climaxing. Her nails dug into his flesh, deeper and sweeter until she whimpered his name and stepped away.

She turned, her lips moist and eyes full of desire. Their gazes met as she stepped away to remove her panties then falling to her knees before him. She freed him from his jeans, stroke him a few times before licking the head. Falcon trembled, looking down at her dark hands wrapped around him. She squeezed perfectly before tugging and when he tensed, Shane pulled him to the back of her throat. Falcon couldn't control himself in that moment. He tried breaking from the cuffs. The urge to wrap his fingers in her hair and push her face down stormed through him. Falcon wanted to feel her throat close tightly around him. He wanted to see her eyes widened and her throat bulged as he filled her mouth and deeper.

"Shane, shit!" Falcon pushed his hips

upward from the floor and she gagged. "You're really…Damn!"

Shane moaned and only sucked him harder.

"You have to let me go," Falcon rasped. "I'm going to…"

Falcon backed off and the minx had the nerve to smirk at him. He struggled with the handcuffs. "Let me go." Falcon demanded.

"Why?"

"I want you."

"You're having me, Falcon. Aren't I satisfying you?" She circled a finger along the head of his member then stuck it between her lips. "I thought you liked it like this."

"I do but…" He trembled then for she was fingering his balls, massaging, squeezing, caressing them. "I'm going to burst."

Shane laughed and went down on him again. This time she took him further, held her throat around him. It was like a vice, squeezing, pulling him to the very edge of his control just before she pulled off and pushed him back to safety. Sweat poured down his face, slid down the center of his back and puddle against the waste of his jeans. Falcon needed her, needed to feel her tight and hot around him. He had to feel her large breasts puddle in his palms as he rode her from behind. Closing his eyes, he gritted his teeth and pulled. The room was suddenly filled with metal separating.

Finally, his hands were free. He couldn't believe it. He'd fought with the cuffs for so long the material came apart and though his wrists burned, Falcon didn't bother checking to see if it had dug into his flesh. Honestly, Falcon was on a carnal mission so a little scratch was not going to get in the way of what he truly hungered for.

Shane gasped and released him but he caught her by the arms and threw her on the couch. Falcon immediately felt like an ass and was about to apologize until he looked down to see she was smiling up at him and touching herself. She stroked her breasts then between her legs to sink a finger in and moaned. Suddenly saying he was sorry evaporated like a puff of smoke in a windstorm and all he could do was wrench his pants from his body. Gripping one of her legs, he twisted and she fell forward, face first into the sofa.

Without even testing her heat, he plunged into her, sinking as deep as he could as hard as he could. She cried out to him and he replied by merely withdrawing and slamming in again. Nothing he'd ever experienced felt as good as that. Nothing he'd ever tasted, or smelled or felt came close to what was pulsing through him. He grabbed her hair, pulled her neck back and fused his lips to hers even as he surged into her hard from behind.

"Yes!" Shane hollered. "Just like that!"

When he released her, it was to brace against her shoulders to get a better leverage. She grunted, whimpered, swore every profanity he'd ever heard. Still, Falcon didn't let up. Even after she orgasmed around him, squeezing him tightly, he continued driving into her. One orgasm led to another and another until she all but melted off his arousal.

He gave her a little breathing room and Shane slipped, like a slinky, to the floor. Her breathing was loud and her shoulders rose and fell rapidly. He met her eyes and he saw mischief there. It was a look no other woman had given him before, one that told him she knew what was coming, she knew the beast she'd unleashed and she hungered to get mauled by him.

Still, Shane backed away from him, smirking as she went.

"Shane," Falcon said. "Do not make me chase you."

"Why not?" She winked. "I thought half the fun is the chase."

"Because I'm about to explode." Falcon admitted. "You made me this hard and you *will* satisfy me."

She grinned, stuck her tongue out at him but kept on crawling backward. Falcon wasn't having it. He stalked her, walking slowly after her. In that moment it was like he was intoxicated. Having her go before he'd had a chance for release was out of the question. He wanted more and she was going to give it to him.

At the bedroom door, he figured they'd played enough games. Falcon, slipped to one knee, grabbed her left ankle and pulled her across the hardwood floor until he was between her legs. He fingered her, using one hand to press into her abdomen to keep her in place. As she writhed against his hands, calling out to him, begging him to give it to her deeper, Falcon smiled. He knew she was almost ready to go again for she tightened around his fingers. Instantly, he withdrew them and replaced them with his hardness.

She climaxed around him causing Falcon's eyes to cross. He was so close. The fire inside him pushed the hot lava of his desires further and further toward the edge. Each time he sank into her, every time she shouted his name, each time her finger nails made tracks down his arms, Falcon knew he was inching closer and closer. Then suddenly, as she arched her back for him and gave herself over once again to a rather spectacular undoing, Falcon lost control. He thrived in the madness her body caused in him and embraced the lunacy with all his soul.

Then it happened. Every muscle in his body tightened and his eyes widened. He stared down at her, beautiful and radiant in her undoing. Her dark nipples tight like Hershey kisses pleaded to be pinched, to be pulled and Falcon gave in to the urges. And just like that, with his head tossed back, Falcon fell apart. He lost every ounce of control that remained within him and he gave himself over to the light that Shane's body sent flashing through him like a beautiful strobe light on a dark Saturday night.

CHAPTER ELEVEN

Rounds two and three happened at the foot of the bed. Each round was hotter than the next, each orgasm more powerful than the ones before. During one session, Falcon had gripped her corset, and tugged. Shane thought for sure she'd be upset but the ruined piece of clothing only made her body hotter. This new wildness in her confused her. By the time Falcon picked Shane up and dropped her to the bed, she was exhausted but still turned on. Instead of behaving, Shane went on all fours to give him a view of what she held so dear between her legs. Falcon didn't give up either and round four and five happened. Thunder crashed across the sky and lightening lit up their room but Shane didn't cower away. Instead, she held onto her man and gave him a part of her no other would have. As she rode the wave of her umpteenth orgasm, Shane knew that no matter what happened the next day, she couldn't let Falcon go. She knew no other man could satisfy her the way he could.

Finally, she flopped to the bed and Falcon fell beside her. They were both breathing hard and covered in sweat. The sheets were damp with their perspiration. Together, they remained still and she listened to the sound of their breathing mingled with the far off roll of thunder. Their night had been perfect. Their passions hot enough to burn though anything and Shane had been happy. The idea that she was probably going to be sore in the morning swam through her head but she quickly silenced it with a yawn.

"Are you okay?" Falcon asked.

"Why wouldn't I be?"

"I wasn't very gentle with you," Falcon said. "I just couldn't…Damn, Shane. I didn't know you like it like that."

She laughed and managed to pull enough strength to lift her head and kiss his shoulder. "Me either," she admitted. "I don't know what came over me."

"Wow."

"I could apologize." Shane yawned. Her hips had already started throbbing from their workout.

"Would you mean it?"

"No."

"Then why say it?"

Shane laughed. She remembered that conversation, only before, it was the other way around. "It would make you feel better."

Falcon chuckled.

They remained there for a while longer—long enough for their breathing to level out and for their bodies to cool down. Shane was the first to stir and sat up. She reached for the phone and put in an order for room service, including a bottle of wine and an ice-cream cake then kissed Falcon's back.

Falcon moaned.

"I'm going to take a shower," Shane said.

"This means I have to listen for the door?"

"Yes."

"This means I have to put pants on?"

Shane laughed. "Yes," she answered again.

"Darling, you're so mean."

"I know, baby." She kissed his neck then hurried into the bathroom.

For a moment after she locked herself in, Shane stared into her eyes in the mirror. All through her sex life she'd never done anything like what she'd done with Falcon before. No man had pulled her hair, spanked her and tore her clothes off. Instead of being angry, instead of wanting him dead, Shane yearned to do it again. She craved climbing back into his bed and misbehaving just so she could feel his large palm falling hard against her ass-cheeks.

That was a part of her that had remained hidden even from herself. Shane had to admit, she liked it. She liked it a lot. The woman who looked back at her in that mirror was different. She was confident, sensual—beautiful. She was the woman Shane always wanted to be and for that revelation to come from Falcon made it even better. Laughing softly to herself, Shane grabbed a bottle of Cherry Blossom scented body wash then stepped into the shower. She washed herself carefully, including her face. Once she was finished, Shane wrapped a towel around her body and brushed her hair straight and back.

By the time she was back in the room, there was a food cart sitting at the foot of the bed and Falcon was sitting, looking down at his cell and her heart stopped.

"The station?" Shane asked.

Falcon looked up. "No. Danielle. She wanted to know what I was doing."

"Oh?" Shane clutched at her towel. "What did you tell her?"

"That I was spending time with you."

"Right."

"You hungry?" Falcon asked, reaching

across to lift the covering from the plates. “Come sit with me and let’s eat something.”

Shane walked over and sat beside him. She curled her legs under her body and accepted the plate he offered. Silently, she ate though suddenly Shane didn’t feel hungry. His fingers were still imprinted in her flesh, she could feel it. It was as if she was sweetly branded by him and no matter how hard Shane tried forgetting, tried to pull it together, Falcon James was in control of her system.

“I’m sorry if I seemed a little weird earlier,” Shane said.

“Weird? About what?”

Shane shrugged. “You on your phone. I know you’re a cop and that’s what you do. I only wanted to spend tonight with you.”

“And we will—I’m not on call tonight. My crew has a few nights off before that comes around again.”

“I can do better.”

Falcon laughed and kissed her head before

going back to his plate. "If you weren't pouting with me leaving after what we've just done to each other then I'd be worried. Trust me, Shane, it's fine."

She smiled and nodded.

More silence. But this time it was a loaded one—one that didn't scare her or made her feel as if she was the loneliest woman on earth. It was filled with memories of Falcon against her, over her and in her. She used that quiet to relive it all, from the couch to the floor to the bed.

"When we tell Danielle," Shane said after clearing her throat. "Did you want to do it alone or would you like me to be there with you?"

"It involves you. I think you should be there."

"I'm still scared."

"I know. So am I. But we can't keep this from her. One day she will walk in on us kissing because I can't keep my hands off you. Then what?" Falcon dragged a cloth napkin over his lips then set his plate on the cart. "I prefer we sit her down and speak to her."

"I'm ready."

Falcon smiled. "Now?"

"No. Maybe tomorrow or whenever." Shane chuckled. "I just—I want you to know you can tell her whenever."

"I never want to deny you, Shane," Falcon said, reaching across to bury his fingers in her hair and inching in. "You deserved to be claimed—every bit of you, every hair on your head, every heave of your breasts—all of it is being claimed. All of you belongs to me."

Usually, if a man said something like that to her, Shane would be furious. Hearing Falcon say it, and seeing the way he looked at her while speaking those words, Shane knew what he meant. He wanted her in private and in public. He will yearn for her in their bed and in the streets and didn't care who knew or saw or heard. Suddenly, Shane felt like the sexiest woman on the face of the earth.

As the night gave way to the wee hours of

the morning, Shane and Falcon snacked on ice-cream cake and watched a movie. This time, they both remained awake through the whole thing. Just before they went to sleep, they made love once more. This time, she opened herself up to soft caresses, tender kisses and feeling her world fall apart with his.

That night, Shane slept better than she had in a long time. She'd slept beside Falcon in the same bed before but nothing compared to having him hold her all night. She sighed, snuggled closer to his large, warm body and closed her eyes once more. Morning came too soon. The sun flowed through cracks in the blinds and the curtains and warmed her. Shane groaned and lifted her head.

"Do you have plans?" Falcon asked.

She turned to see his face. He still had his eyes closed.

"I have to go in later to relieve Anisa at the store," Shane said, dragging a finger against his lips. "She has an exam tonight. I offered to work for her this morning but she has a girlfriend now so she needs the extra money."

"I see…" Falcon opened his beautiful, grey gaze then and smiled. "Okay. I have a shift later. I'm hoping it stays quiet since I won't be working with my team."

"How comes?"

"The captain of the Five twenty was shot while on duty a few weeks ago. The other captains are taking turns covering for him until he's back on his feet."

Shane sighed. "I hope that will be soon. Didn't he have a second in command?"

"He did—the second in command is the person who shot him."

"What?" Shane was incredulous. "Are you kidding me?"

"No. I want to think it wasn't on purpose—that they just got their lines crossed and it was friendly fire. But the investigation is ongoing and so far everyone is tightlipped about it."

"Well, we can hope for the best." She fell back to the pillow beside him. "Isn't it strange commanding a crew you barely know?"

"It is. But I'll be okay. How are you feeling?"

"Sore," Shane admitted.

"Damn, I'm sorry, sweetheart."

"Are you kidding?" Shane asked, dropping a kiss to Falcon's lips. "I wouldn't have it any other way."

When they finally emerged from the hotel later, around lunch time, it wasn't because either of them particularly wanted to. Shane pouted the whole time she got dressed and Falcon merely reclined against the headboards, muscular arms folded behind his head, grinning at her.

In the sunlight, Shane opened the back door so Falcon could drop her bag on the seat then closed it and joined him at the front of the car. She stood before him, her body pressing into his and clutching his elbows. He kissed her then lifted his head. "I'll see you later?"

Shane shrugged. "Not sure. Depends on the accounting after I close up. Earliest tomorrow."

"I could make us some dinner and we could tell the kidlet about us." Falcon suggested.

Shane nodded. "Sounds like a plan." She pushed to her tip toes to kiss him again.

"In the meantime I'll call you tonight to uh—well—tuck you in?"

"Tuck me in?" Shane giggled. "I highly doubt that."

"Well, I'm a man of many surprises, Shane. I'll talk to you later."

She kissed him twice more before stepping from his arms. "See you, Birdman."

Shane moved around him to pull open her car door. Though Falcon backed up to give her room to reverse from the spot, he didn't walk away. She waved at him, turned her car for the exit to the parking lot and kept her eyes on him through her rearview for as long as she could. As he became smaller in the mirror, Shane switched her eyes to the road ahead. She couldn't help thinking of him as a powerful force, one that had been under her nose all along. One that had been by her side but she had her friendship shades on and just couldn't see him for what he could mean in her life.

Though she was close with her sister, Shane didn't know if she should go in depth about what happened between her and Falcon when they made love. How could she explain how animalistic things became? Would Francine understand? But the truth was, Shane had to talk to someone she trusted about it and Jana was not the person.

Muttering under her breath, she used her hands free to call her sister.

"Detective Teller."

"Hello, Detective. This is your sister calling."

Francine laughed. "Hey sis. How are you?"

"Sore—you got like an hour to have lunch with your sister?"

Francine paused then cleared her throat. "Sure. Actually, I got two. Want me to meet you somewhere?"

"Nope. I'm on my way to pick you up now."

"Okay. I'll be ready."

Excitement caused Shane to press her foot down a little harder on the gas and she made it to her sister's station in a few minutes. True to form, Francine was out front, sitting on a low wall, waiting for her. When her sister got into the car, Shane reached over and hugged her tightly then groaned at the tenderness in her body.

"Lawd-ha-mercy," Francine said. "What were the two of you doing last night?"

Shane switched the car into drive, checked her mirrors and blindspots then pulled from the curb. "What didn't we do?"

Francine laughed. "Okay, before you start, can we go down to Food Truck Alley? I'm craving that duck fat poutine."

Shane made a face. "Sure."

"Okay, now talk to me."

"Well," Shane said. "You know how I had plans at the hotel to use the spa and just breathe. I invited Falcon to come and I went to that lingerie fitting appointment you made for me and got something nice."

"Sweet. I have to see it!"

"Can't."

"What'd you mean can't? You're my sister and I've seen you naked, so of course I can."

"That's not why I said you can't see it," Shane said. "You can't see it because Falcon shredded it."

"Whoa! What?"

"He got impatient with all the little strings and bows and ripped it off," Shane explained with a shiver. "I'm telling you Francine the man's a beast."

"In all the right ways, right?"

Shane nodded as she made the left turn down Porter Crescent that would carry them down to the lake and a small area dubbed *Food Truck Alley.* "He's into handcuffs and blindfolds and…"

"But you're not into all those things…"

"I didn't think so. But turns out I am. And

then there are the spankings…"

"Say what now?"

"Great, you think I'm weird." Shane sighed.

"No. I don't think you're weird. I'm just surprised. Well, wait, no. Now that I think about it, Falcon does look like the kind of man to take charge. And he is a cop so a fetish for cuffs isn't that far off. But you do enjoy being with him like this?"

Shane's heart did a little flip and she smiled. "Yes. Last night I lost count how many times we went at it. And the orgasms—Lord."

"Plural? More than one?"

"Oh honey. I lost count."

Francine whistled. "For a woman who never had a big O with a man before, Falcon must be damn good."

Shane pulled into a parking spot closest to the food truck she knew her sister liked and killed the engine. "So good."

They scrambled from the car and made their way over to *Fatty Delight*. Once her sister had her poutine, they wandered along the alley, through other people, past a few other trucks until they arrived at *Bollywood Salsa*. It was a food truck that served a kind of Indian Mexican blend. She ordered the tandoori chicken tacos and the two then found a seat on a surprisingly empty park bench.

"So, you two taking it to the next level?" Francine asked.

"We are." Shane bit into one of her tacos and moaned at the explosion of fantastic flavours. She chewed silently before continuing. "We're making dinner at his place tomorrow so we can tell Danielle."

"She knows, you know?" Francine asked. "I don't even know why you two think you could hide something like that from her."

"We weren't hiding it. Falcon and I decided to wait until our relationship was a little more—on stronger footing before we tell her. And did she say something?"

"No. She's been asking me if I think you'd

want to be her mom. She even showed me that gown she's designing. The kid's got talent."

"Of course I'd want to be her mother!" Shane muttered around a mouthful of taco. "She's beautiful and talented and kind—I just—I don't know. A little girl deserves her real mother."

"No. A little girl deserves the mother who deserves her. A woman doesn't have to give birth to be a mother—hell any woman out there can give birth. But it takes a strong female to be a true *mother.*"

Shane nodded in agreement but said nothing else.

"So." Francine prodded. "You can say it. It's okay."

"Say what?"

"You were right Francine. Falcon James does rock my world."

Shane groaned. "Seriously?"

"Say it! Make mamma happy!"

"Fine." Shane groaned. "You were right. Falcon James does rock my world!"

"Boom bitches!" Francine cheered.

Her sudden outburst startled a woman who was sitting at a nearby table. She glared at Shane and Francine. Shane covered her face and shook her head. "See? This is why I can't take you to nice places."

Francine giggled. "I don't care." She leaned in to whisper. "Shane and Falcon sitting in a tree!"

CHAPTER TWELVE

"Dad?"

"Yeah, sweetie?"

"Are you okay?" Danielle asked.

"Of course! Why do you ask?"

"You just put the flour in the fridge and the margarine in the cupboard."

Falcon shook his head and pulled open the fridge. She was right. Shaking his head, he pulled the container with the flour out and switched the products to go in the right place.

"Are you sure, you're okay?" Danielle asked.

He looked over at her. Concern filled her beautiful face. "Yeah. I'm fine. I just have a lot on my mind."

"Anything I can help with?"

Falcon shook his head. "Nah. It's just stuff. Are you finished your English homework?"

"Yup. All done. Ready to spend a quiet night with you and Godie."

Honestly, Falcon was nervous. Though he told Shane not to worry about anything he just couldn't shake his own trepidations. Still, he managed to push all that aside and spent a few hours with his daughter cooking dinner for when Shane arrived. The closer it came to that time, is the more he dreaded it and he didn't know why. Danielle loved Shane, there were no questions about that.

Finally Shane arrived and Danielle admitted her into the house. Falcon hurried up the stairs to change his shirt since he'd managed to get gravy all over it. When he returned, Danielle and Shane were busy setting the table.

"Hey Birdman." Shane greeted him.

"Hi." He couldn't manage another word. She was dressed in a pencil skirt that hugged her curves, a white top that though he couldn't see through, showed off her ample breasts and her hair was tied up in a simple pony tail that left great access to her neck. Falcon bit back on the groan that threatened to seep from his lips even as he folded his arms to keep from reaching for her. He wanted to kiss her then, to feel her red lips against his, to taste the cherry of her lipstick.

"Danielle," Falcon said, softly. "Sit down for a second. Shane and I have something we need to tell you."

"Um…" Danielle looked from Falcon to Shane but fell into a nearby chair.

Falcon pulled out another chair from the table, and turned it so he could be face to face with her as he delivered the news. "You know, that—um—you have your mother, right? And no one will ever replace her for you, I know that. But it's been a few years since she's been gone and I think it's safe to assume she's…"

"…Not coming back." Danielle interrupted. "I know that."

"Shane and I…um…" Falcon stopped and

glanced up at Shane who smiled at him softly and he trembled. "Shane and I are sort of seeing each other."

"Really?" Danielle looked up at Shane then met Falcon's eyes again. "What do you mean sort of?"

"We wanted to make sure it wasn't just a fluke before we said anything to you," Shane said. "We didn't want to pull you into it if we weren't serious about being together."

"So, in other words, you're sleeping together."

Falcon scratched the back of his neck. Suddenly the room had gotten so warm, he could barely stand it. "Yes."

Silence.

Falcon felt as if the world was falling into an abyss and he was the only one who knew. Even so, as much as he wanted to scream to get up and walk away, as a father, he couldn't. Danielle needed time to digest what they'd just told her and he couldn't rush her.

"Are you two going to get married?" Danielle asked.

"Um…" Shane said.

"One day," Falcon assisted. "Not tomorrow or even a year from now. Relationships take time and we want to spend that time getting to know each other and…"

"But you know each other," Danielle said. "You've been best friends since the womb."

Shane laughed. "Yes but we know each other as friends. Making the jump to lovers is a completely different kind of relationship."

"So, is that what you are now, lovers?"

Falcon nodded. "Yes."

"Oh, okay," Danielle said. "Cool."

Falcon arched a brow. "So? What do you think?"

"Dad, honestly, mom left and you turned into a hermit." Danielle replied. "You haven't dated. You haven't brought anyone home—nothing. I would have been happy for you to be dating again. It's just kinda awesome that it's

Godie."

Shane laughed and Falcon chuckled.

"What you're saying, Danielle, is you're okay with your dad and I being together."

"More than okay." Danielle rose to frame Shane's face with her palms. "I was saying to Aunt Francine when I was with her that you two are just wasting valuable time not trying to date or something. Don't worry. If I was going to get a new mother, I'm happy it's you."

Shane hugged Danielle then and Falcon flopped back into his chair. The relief he felt left him drained as his lower back pulsed against the chair. Danielle walked over to kiss his forehead then hugged him and Falcon could only hang on to her while meeting Shane's eyes. The moment Danielle released him, he rose and did precisely what he'd wanted to do since she walked into the house. He kissed her, deeply, passionately.

"Aww you two!" Danielle groaned. "Get a room! I'm going upstairs to call Charlie, let me know when it's safe to come back."

Falcon laughed.

"It's safe! We'll eat, set the dishes in the dishwasher then you can call Charlie. Deal?"

Danielle crinkled her nose but shook Shane's hand. "Deal."

All through dinner, the three discussed what life was going to be like from then on. Danielle was curious if Shane would move in with them and Falcon had to agree with Shane when she said, not yet. He didn't want to rush into anything. Then again, his father always told him that love doesn't work on humanity's timeline. It comes when he wants and there was nothing anyone could do about it. He'd rushed into things with Shannon and it only ended in tears.

No, Shane deserved better and he would see to it that she got it.

When dinner was finally over, Danielle stocked the dishwasher, turned it on then darted up the stairs. Falcon assumed it was to gossip with Charlie about Falcon dating Shane. He smiled and leaned into the doorframe, watching

Shane put away what was left of their dinner. She carefully scraped the leftovers into smaller containers, stashed them in the fridge then set the pots in the sink.

"Leave those," Falcon told her. "I can do them later."

"If we leave them the food will get stuck and then it will be hell cleaning them."

Falcon groaned and walked over to help her with the pots. He figured the sooner she was finished the faster he could sneak her out of the house for a walk and maybe a little something extra. They couldn't do anything with Danielle around.

"Want to go for a drive with me?" Falcon asked. He washed the first pot and gave it to her for a rinse.

"Are you going to take me to the make-out spot and try getting to second base, Falcon James?"

He laughed out loud. "You know all my tricks." He kissed her.

"I have to warn you. I'm not easy."

Falcon licked his lips and reached for the next dirty pot. "You're not?" He sighed dramatically with a smirk. "I guess I have to make it worth your while then."

"You guessed right."

"Okay...." Falcon finished the final pot and rinsed it himself. Once they were done, wrapped his fingers against the back of her neck and kissed her. This time he took his time to taste her tongue and nibble on her bottom lip before plunging his tongue into her mouth. She moaned and melted into his chest and Falcon released her. If he hadn't they wouldn't be able to stop. Inhaling, he rubbed is hands up and down her arms and locked gaze with Shane.

"Elle?" He hollered.

"Yeah dad?" Danielle answered from upstairs.

"Shane and I are going for a drive," Falcon reported. "I assume you're still talking to Charlie?"

"Yup. Have fun," Danielle hollered down the stairs. "And Shane?"

"Yeah sweetie?"

"Can you get me some – um – you know?" Shane looked at Falcon and shrugged before stepping from his arms. She headed for the stairs and Falcon followed in time to see her jogging up.

Falcon stood at the foot of the stairs and watched as his teenage daughter whispered into Shane's ear. He was pretty sure he knew what she wanted. After all, he was her father and she was at that age. But Danielle had always been embarrassed to ask him for tampons. Over the years, he'd tried paying Shane back for all the ones she'd bought for Danielle but Shane would merely frown at him and walk away. When she returned, he smiled at her and grabbed his car keys. He wrapped his arm around her rounded hips and led her through the front door, stopping long enough to lock it behind them.

They drove in silence for about twenty minutes. They passed Shane's wedding dress store and continued. They stopped long enough for Shane to pick up tampons for her god-daughter. She stashed them in her purse on the back seat and soon they were on their way once more. Shane sighed and relaxed into the leather of the front seat. Falcon reached across and laced his fingers with hers. She was amaze at how good that felt. It was a simple action, something she shouldn't really read too much into. But how could she not? Falcon's large hand was gentle against hers—he was warm and strong. Those were two of the things her mother always told her to look for in a man.

She didn't speak, only lifted their hands and kissed the back of his. He parked the vehicle in the lot of their favorite ice-cream shop and Shane had to laugh. "We didn't have to come all the way here just because I was having a craving."

"Yes we did." Falcon said pushing from the

car and running around to meet her on the other side. He kissed the side of her head as he wrapped his arm around her hip.

Inside, they made their orders and Shane rested her back against his chest while they waited. Falcon nibbled on her shoulder. A few people walked by and gave them strange looks but she merely grinned. She waved at a few of them and that made them gasp and hurry off. "You'd think they hadn't seen a man kissing a woman before." Shane frowned.

By the time their ice-cream was ready, Shane was trembling in Falcon's arms. Her knees were putty and no matter how hard she tried to pull it together, making her mind focus was much easier said than done. Still, she managed to wrap her fingers around the cone and took a lick.

She allowed Falcon to escort her back to his vehicle and they drove a short distance to the lake where he reversed so the back of the car was facing the view. He helped her up so she could sit on the hood and rest her back into the glass then climbed up beside her. She snuggled into his chest and relaxed.

"It's so nice down here now." Shane sighed. "You know I've never been down here with a man before?"

"What? For real?"

"Seriously. I figured the man who brought me here had to be someone I was serious about."

"Why's that?"

Shane shrugged. "I don't know. Maybe it was because I thought this was as close to heaven as I'd get. Or maybe because of how peaceful it has always been down here. I really can't say." Shane licked at her ice-cream again then sat up to look into Falcon's eyes. "Can I be honest?"

"Of course."

"After, douchebag left, I was broken." Shane admitted. "I know—I know I said I was fine but I was falling apart. I spent numerous nights lying alone in bed sobbing, wondering why I wasn't good enough, why I couldn't keep anyone. For three days I didn't eat anything. I stayed in bed.

When I finally managed to pull myself together—kind of—I spent hours in front of the mirror dissecting every bulge, obsessing over every imperfection. Then I'd go back to bed. I ran the shop when I had to, when Anisa was off but that was about it."

"Why didn't you tell me?"

"You had enough on your plate. You were raising a teenager and working a job that's stressful in itself. I didn't want to add to that. I didn't want to be a burden. Besides, I was always strong Shade. Shane who could fight everyone else's battle for them and here I was letting some asshole with a God complex break me."

"But you were my girl, Shane," Falcon said, his voice cracking. "I would've helped you. There was no reason for you to have gone through that alone."

"I didn't see it that way. I thought you wouldn't want to see me like that. That you would think I was weak."

"That's bullshit, Shane and you know it.

Don't you know how much I love you? You've had my back through everything. When my marriage fell apart who was there to pick up the pieces? When Danielle first started seeing her period and I thought I was going to lose my mind, who stepped in and made sure I knew what I needed to know? And when my baby needs a mother figure in her life because let's face it, there are some things she doesn't want to talk to me about, who steps in time and time again? Shane, you've been a part of my life forever and don't you ever go through something like that again and not tell me! Do you hear me?"

Shane smiled and caressed one side of his face. "I'm sorry, baby. I really am. I'm sorry."

Falcon set his jaw in that determined way that told Shane he was angry with her. Though he bowed his head and pressed his forehead to hers, showing her some tenderness, she knew he was still upset. His brows were still knitted—Shane felt it—and his lips were still drawn into a thin line. Shane brushed her lips against his, periodically sticking her tongue out to lick at him. She dropped her ice-cream to the ground and climb astride his lap. "Forgive me?"

Shane nibbled at his bottom lip, tangled her arms around his neck and dragged her teeth down until she landed against his shoulder. He slid his arms around her and Shane knew she was one step closer to having him smiling into her face as he did unspeakably naughty things to her body.

"Tell me you forgive me," she whispered, grinding down against him, feeling Falcon hard and rising between her legs. "Show me that you forgive me."

Falcon snaked his fingers up her back, teasing her spine before tracing the flesh against her neck. Shane gasped and found his lips. She couldn't kiss him right away for he was touching her, stroking her all the while grinding up against her. When she finally gave him her mouth, it was to the hottest kiss they'd shared yet. Their hot breaths mingled while threatening to drive her crazy. Falcon pulled her hair tie out and tossed it before grabbing a handful of her hair and pressing her head forward. Moaning, Shane slipped a hand between their bodies to fondle him, to feel his hardness throb through the material of his boxers and his pants.

"I need you, Shane," Falcon confessed. "Right here. Right now."

"Falcon..."

"Are you scared?"

"A little."

"Close your eyes." Falcon slipped a hand under her skirt. He gripped the seat of her panties and tugged. The cool lake air washed over her intimately and Shane moaned. "Don't think. Just feel."

He was nibbling against her neck even as he said these words. Shane exhaled long and hard. Pushing to her knees astride his lap, Shane pulled his zipper down then shoved her hand past his fly and into his boxers. Falcon hissed loudly and throbbed hotly in her bare palm. She met his gaze even as she used her free hand to tug at her panties. It took some doing but Shane managed to rip the material before easing to her knees and finding her entrance with his hardness. She kissed him again while pressing down on him, taking him slowly, deeply.

Falcon growled, clutched at her hips to hold them in place then drove his hips roughly upward. Shane couldn't stop it. She couldn't keep her pleasure, the happiness that caused in her inside. She dug her nails into his shoulders. Rolling her hips, Shane tried rejecting the pulsing end she knew was coming. She pressed her face into Falcon's neck, inhaling his scent and getting even more turned on than she thought possible. Her heart raced. Sweat dripped down the center of her back under her clothes.

Then Falcon lifted her skirt to her hips, exposing her to the lake air and the moonlight. He brought his large hand down hard against one cheek and all thoughts of holding off disappeared. Letting her head fall forward, she sank her teeth into his shoulder as her first orgasm of the night raged through her. It curled her toes, caused her whole body to stiffen then trembled like she was a leaf high in the sky. She twisted, floated, danced all the way to the ground for Falcon.

But before she could catch her breath, Falcon was pushing her again, twisting her nipples between his thumbs and forefingers, licking at her neck. Shane had become delirious all over again. All she seemed to be able to do, was toss her head back, give him complete access to her body and ride him as if her life depended on it. The vehicle creaked beneath their rocking bodies. From somewhere deep in her carnal haze she could hear it. But Shane didn't care. Falcon was doing things to her body that she was pretty sure she'd never get for another man.

"You're mine," Shane whispered. "All mine..."

"Shane."

The sound of his voice, raspy and tumbling over her name was like the best aphrodisiac she'd ever experienced. Her whole word exploded in an array of light and fire.

"Say it again." Shane pleaded, breathily. "Say my name?"

He kissed her chin, her cheeks then her forehead. "Shane."

"Yes!" She hissed.

Her body betrayed her once more but this time, she took him with her. This time, he sunk his fingers into her thighs, dragged a hand to the small of her back and pressed. He trapped her over him, buried deeply inside her body. She whimpered, clung to Falcon with all her might.

He's mine. All mine.

Chapter Thirteen

Falcon handed his gun over to be checked and pulled the flaps holding his helmet loose. He removed it and dragged a gloved hand over his head. He had to shoot the bad guy and though the department frowned on that, they would rather every cop go home alive. It couldn't have been helped. Falcon figured it would make the brass feel better because though one of the badguys died, the team had captured the target. The dead perp was just an ass who decided to protect his boss by pulling a gun on cops.

"Eh, Falco!"

He turned and grinned at Detective Francine Teller. He approached her and hugged her tightly. "This one of yours?" he asked.

Francine grinned widely at him and nodded. "Oh yeah. Thank your team for me. We're taking a major baddie off the streets, my friend."

"Yeah."

"So…you and Shane, eh?"

"Yup. Shane and I…"

"Do you love her?"

"Yes."

"Dude, I know you love her," Francine said, tilting her head. "But do you *love* her?"

Falcon frowned. "Yes. I *love* her."

"Have you told her?" Francine asked.

Falcon shook his head. "I can't. Not yet. When I say it, I need her to know that I'm sure. She thinks these things take time so I will show her every day until I feel it's right to say it."

"That's all you can do, man."

"It sucks not being able to tell her." Falcon and Francine walked toward the unit's truck. He tossed his helmet into the carrier and faced her. "I almost said it last night."

"During sex?"

"Yeah. But it's fine. We'll figure this out. We told Danielle and she's good with it."

"Well, that's the battle right there."

Falcon laughed. "I don't want to hurt her, Franny. It would kill me. I'm trying my best do this right. I don't want to be that man again where the woman feels he's not good enough and leaves. I mean, I know Shane and she'd never do that but I don't want to make her unhappy either."

"I hear the way she talks about you, Falco. You have nothing to worry about. Shane's always been that woman who will have your back as long as you show her the same, you know? She isn't going anywhere, especially away from you and Dani. So stop focusing on that and latch on to making each other happy. You know, in a little while Danielle will be off to university of college and the two of you will have to be happy on your own."

Falcon cringed. The thought of his baby leaving for post secondary education scared him. But it had to happen. "Truth."

"Damn right, truth. Listen, I gatta take him

in. A few of your guys coming for the escort?"

"Yeah. Belle and Dawson will ride. They know that already."

"Good. Come by my place tonight. Bring Danielle and Shane." Francine looked around. "Invite your guys. We're going to be carnivores and drink beer. Whatdya say?"

"I say you're speaking my language. What time?"

"Eight? It's Friday night and I don't know if you guys have plans..."

Falcon shook his head. "No plans. Danielle may have something with Charlie..."

"Bring him along too. Let's have a good old fashion blow out."

"All right. We'll see you later."

The two hugged and he watched her check on the prisoner then climbed behind the wheel of her vehicle. He remained where he was standing until the vehicles pulled out of the parking lot before climbing into the truck with the others and locking the door. Topaz immediately leaned forward.

"You seem happier," Topaz said.

"Yeah. Shane and I are officially a thing."

"Booyah!" Topaz cheered.

The others in the truck turned their heads to look at him. Falcon laughed and Topaz shook his head.

"Sorry," he said with a small wave. "So, you guys are happy then?"

Falcon nodded. "Yeah. Even told Danielle." He went on to tell Topaz the whole story about how scared he had been but once he saw Danielle's reaction everything was good. He even divulged their night out by the lake on the trunk of this car. Topaz grinned.

"You see? I told you that it wasn't you," Topaz said. "When Shannon left, it was all her, brother. All her."

Falcon patted Topaz's shoulder and the two of them sat back in silence for the rest of the ride back to the station. The ride was bumpier than he remembered so he turned his head to look out the front of the carrier. The morning sun had changed to just after lunchtime sun and Falcon could feel the shift in temperature. In the distance, the clouds were dark and he prayed it wouldn't rain. He had this desperate need to be around people who cared for him. Perhaps it was seeing how one man's life could be over and his freedom disappeared. Maybe that was pushing him into a state of melancholy only hugs from Danielle and kisses from Shane could cure.

Once they arrived at the station, he gathered everyone in the meeting room. By time Dawson and Belle had returned. He gave them the invite to Francine's but only Topaz and Belle took the offer. The others had a baseball game they had tickets for. He told them the time and reminded them of the address then grabbed his gear. He stashed everything away before changing into a pair of jeans and a graphic shirt.

Falcon wasn't really paying attention for the drive. All he knew was he had to go somewhere to breathe. When he looked up, he was parked in a spot across the street from Shane's store. Falcon smiled, unlatched his seatbelt and climbed from the front of his truck. After looking both ways, he jogged across and let himself into the quaint store.

"Welcome to…Falcon!" Shane dashed around the counter and tossed herself into his arms. "How'd it go? How's Francine?"

"It went well. Franny is okay. She's inviting us over to her place tonight. It's going to be a party." He kissed her, tapped her bum playfully and released her before one of her clients barged in or something.

Shane giggled. "Falcon, you behave yourself."

He wiggled his brows at her even as he reached in for another kiss. "So? Are we going?"

"I wanted to have you all to myself but I can't be selfish." She pouted prettily. "We should go. It makes Franny happy to see all of us after she finishes a big case like this one."

"Okay, good."

"What's up? What brings you down here? Looking for a dress?"

Falcon glanced around with a laugh. "I doubt any of these would match my eyes. I wanted to see you. Can you take a few minutes?"

"No. Anisa isn't due in for another hour and I have to finish cataloging some accessories. If you wanted to hang around I could treat you to lunch?"

Falcon felt his heart rise then. "What kind of lunch?"

"Falcon James you get your mind out of the gutter!" She swatted him.

That only made Falcon laugh harder. "I can't help it. You're very sexy."

Shane giggled. "Think we'd have some time before we have to go to Franny's later? I'm talking *alone* time."

"We should. Danielle is heading to Charlie's later. I still have to call and ask her if they want to come to this party. Though I don't think she would because her and Charlie would be the only two their age there."

"True. Well, if Danielle declines our invite, I have a plan for you."

Falcon moaned. "Does it involve you very naked?"

"Maybe." She took his hand and led him to a comfortable, white sofa on the far side of the store. "Sit. Let me work."

"Sure." But Falcon was busy looking around. He chewed on his bottom lip when he noticed there were cameras in the store. He groaned not sure why he thought there weren't any—then again it could have only been his hope.

"Your daughter is talented."

"Oh yeah?"

"She emailed me the dress she designed for my store," Shane explained.

Falcon watched her tapped away at the laptop beside the cash registered. She then picked up the portable computer and carried it over and fell into the seat beside him. When she turned the screen Falcon was stunned. The gown was beautiful and his baby had designed it.

"Wow – Danielle – *my* Danielle did that?"

Shane nodded. "She has an eye, Falcon. She really does."

"Wow. That talent didn't come from me and it definitely didn't come from her mother."

Shane laughed.

"So, are you going to produce it?"

"Yeah. Her and I had a deal."

"Shane?"

"Hmm?"

"Do we have to wait until Anisa gets here?"

Before she could answer, the small chime above the door sounded. Falcon could kill anyone who walked in at that precise moment. He'd wanted to take her into his arms, to feel her warm and trembling against him. He wasn't sure why the sensation was that strong. Instead of committing a felony, he inhaled deeply and watched her rise to greet the newcomers.

Feeling out of place, Falcon walked over to kiss her head. "I'll come back in an hour."

“Where are you going?” Shane asked.

“Not sure yet. I’m thinking Danielle needs supplies to continue designing.”

Shane smiled. “See you in an hour baby.”

He nodded and just before he stepped out the door, he heard a part of her conversation with the bride to be.

“Is that your man?” The woman asked.

“Yes,” Shane replied without hesitation.

That was all Falcon needed to hear for his heart to do summersaults as he stepped into the late afternoon sunlight.

EPILOGUE – Six months later

Falcon climbed from the front seat of his truck. He reached into the back to grab a bunch of red roses before closing the door and glancing both ways. Seeing the way clear, he jogged across the street and let himself into Shane's brand new store. She'd finally decided to open a second store and give the reigns of it over to Anisa. She didn't have to hire anyone because Danielle offered to accept the job and would work there for the summer until it was time to begin classes at the Fashion Institute.

"Baby!" Shane waved. "I didn't expect you to come by."

He kissed her and offered her the flowers after removing one. That one he gave to Anisa who giggled, sniffed the rose and hugged him.

When they were alone, he braced his back to

the counter and leveled his eyes on her. He loved the way she enjoyed the small things in life. Though she had money, Shane never turned her nose up at the paintings Danielle did over the past few months or the flowers he brought her. Instead, she sniffed them, caressed their petals with a gentle finger then beamed beautifully at him.

"Are you going to pick up Danielle and Charlie at the airport?"

Falcon nodded. "Yeah."

"I miss her," Shane said. "It hasn't been the same since she decided to go travelling. I've been worried the whole time."

"I know, sweetie." Falcon rubbed her back. "You tossed and turned so much at nights I would wake up and hold you."

"Sorry."

"Don't be. She's your baby too. I'd be concerned if you weren't worried."

"Falcon, do you want more kids?"

"Um..."

"I mean I know Danielle is almost an adult—hell come October she'll be eighteen. But I haven't had any kids yet and I would like to have at least one."

"More children, with you? Of course."

"Don't just say that. You have to mean it too."

Falcon caressed her cheek gently. "Carl Sandberg said that a baby is God's opinion that the world should go on."

"And you believe this Sandberg is right?"

"Oh, I know he is. I'm thirty five years old, Shane." Falcon kissed her. "I had Danielle young and she was a blessing in my life. Having a child with you would be nothing less than that."

Shane hugged him tightly. "You've made me so happy."

"I'm glad." Falcon kissed her head. "What about Danielle—it wouldn't make much sense starting the adoption process. She'll be eighteen soon."

"I don't need a piece of paper to tell me she's

my baby," Shane said, irritation evident in her voice. "She's always been a part of my heart—us being together will only make it, you know, better."

Falcon chuckled. "I'm sorry darling." He tapped the tip of her nose with his right index finger. "Now, I have to go get our child before the traffic gets bad heading into the airport. I know you wanted to come along but since you're filling in for Anisa...Have you given any thought to hiring someone to help out? I mean it's unrealistic to think she can run this place by herself with a volunteer."

"I have and I gave her the go ahead to do that. She's interviewing candidates from the Fashion Institute starting tomorrow. It would be nice to have someone into fashion work here." Shane looked around. "I think she should hire two—what'd you think?"

"I think you're right. That way she can take some time off with customers and focus on everything else that she has doing to run this place."

Shane grinned. "I love bouncing ideas off you." She stopped speaking and darkness clouded her eyes.

"Something wrong?" Falcon asked.

"I love you, Falcon."

Falcon tilted his head as silence wrapped itself around them. Perhaps he imagined it and Shane hadn't said anything at all.

"Falcon?"

"Y-yeah?"

"Did you hear me?"

"I thought I was imagining it—what did you say? Just so I know."

Shane set the flowers on the counter behind him and stood before him. She lifted her face and for the first time, Falcon saw the tears just simmering under the surface. Her eyes danced at him. "I love you, Falcon."

Unsure what to do with his hands, Falcon rested them on her hips the leaned heavily to the counter behind him. Hearing her say those three, little words did something magical to every fiber of his being. "Don't say it unless you mean it," Falcon pleaded. "I couldn't stand it if you didn't."

Shane smiled. "I love you."

With a helpless sigh, Falcon cradled her face and kissed her. He trembled as her arms circled him. He was powerless to the sensation she sent through him and Falcon was beyond trying to control anything. "I love you too," he said around kisses. "I didn't want to say anything just in case you thought it was too soon."

"I thought that," Shane admitted, smoothing her palms against the front of his shirt. "But screw it! I don't want to be afraid anymore. I don't want to hide anything from you. I've tried that and you yelled at me."

She pouted beautifully at him and Falcon melted and kissed her protruding lips.

"I'm sorry, baby." His voice cracked. "I never want you to feel as if you have to hide anything from me—not your passion in my bed, not when you're feeling broken and especially not your love."

"It's going to take some getting used to. But I'll do better."

Falcon hugged her then. He hung onto her the slid his hands down to cup her ass. Her cheeks were supple in his grip and he couldn't help remembering how they felt as his palms fell against them to make her squirm. "When you get home tonight," Falcon said.

"I'm all yours."

Falcon moaned. "Precisely."

"I'll hurry home."

He kissed her again, feeling her lips mould with his. Reluctantly, he stepped away from her and headed for the door. "I'll be waiting, Shane. Don't be late."

"And what if I am?"

Falcon laughed and turned to look at her. "Are you hankering for a spanking, Shane?"

She winked at him. "We'll see."

With smile, Falcon stepped through the

doors and into the dying sun. He crossed the street and stood with his back against the driver's side of his truck, watching the store. He truly hoped Shane would be late. If he was being honest, he would admit bending her over his knees did something wild to him. Even as he climbed behind the wheel, he couldn't stop smiling. Shane Teller loved him and that night, after he had his fill of her delectable body, he was going to pop the question. One day soon, Shane Teller would become Shane James and then she would truly be all his.

Feeling as if he was walking on air, Falcon turned the truck north.

The End

ABOUT THE AUTHOR

Born in Kingston, Jamaica, Kadian Tracey moved to Canada as a freshly minted teenager. She always had her nose buried in a book - from Mystery to romance, Kadian read it all.

Writing also under Kendra Mei Chailyn, Kadian has a few titles under her belt, including, COWBOY LULLABY, BOKEN WINGS, MADE TO BEND NOT BREAK, the SHADOWCAT series, WHAT YOU DO TO ME and others.

With a love of words and art, Kadian loves photography, writing, travelling, cooking, eating (of course), Blue Jays baseball and spending time with family and friends. You can find her on twitter @Kendramechailyn, and on facebook!

ALSO BY THE AUTHOR

Writing as Kadian Tracey

Shadowcat Series:

Re's Curse

Re's Redemption

A Lover's Wish

Broken Wings

Cowboy Lullaby

Made to Bend, Not Break

Writing As Kendra Mei Chailyn

Made to Love You

Loving Jo

What You Do To Me

Kiss It Better

60314022R00148

Made in the USA
Charleston, SC
27 August 2016